Also by Mark Greathouse

The Wolf's Tales

The Wolf's Quest: Isa's Adventure Begins

The Frontier Chronicles

Perilous Trails: Jack's Adventure Begins

Wyoming Calls: Jack's Risky Quest

Longhorns North: Jack's Great Trail Drive

Warpath: Jack's Faith is Tested

Hunter Vs. Hunted: Jack's Great Frontier Challenge

Freedom Drovers: Jack's Awesome Crusade

A Poison Spreads: Jack Seeks the Antidote

Darkness Looms: Jack Faces War

The Tumbleweed Sagas

Nueces Justice

Nueces Reprise

Nueces Deceit

Nueces Blood

Nueces Grit

Nueces Truth

Nueces Legend

The Tumbleweed Sagas - Junior's Story

Lone Star Vigilante

Guns on the Guadalupe

Railroad to Perdition

Nicholas Dunn: The Making of a Texas Legend (A Western Adventure)

The Frontier Calls: Two Souls, One Adventure

The Frontier Calls: Two Souls, One Adventure

The Wolf's Tales

Book Two

Mark Greathouse

The Frontier Calls: Two Souls, One Adventure
Paperback Edition

WISE WOLF BOOKS
An Imprint of Wolfpack Publishing
1707 E. Diana Street
Tampa, FL 33610

wisewolfbooks.com

Paperback ISBN 978-1-968733-33-9 eBook ISBN 978-1-968733-32-2

Dedicated with love to my wife Carolyn, our two sons Mike and Matt.

Love is patient, love is kind. It does not envy, it does not boast, it is not proud. It does not dishonor others, it is not self-seeking, it is not easily angered, it keeps no record of wrongs. Love does not delight in evil but rejoices with the truth. It always protects, always trusts, always hopes, always perseveres..

—1 Corinthians 13:4-7

*For we too were once foolish, disobedient, deceived, enslaved by various passions and pleasures, living in malice and envy, hateful, detesting one a*nother.

—Titus 3:3

The Cast

The Cast

Isa (a.k.a. Wolf) O'Toole—*Sixteen-year-old son of Jack O'Toole, whose quest is to venture alone into the great frontier of the North Platte River country. Isa translates to wolf in the Comanche tongue.*

Awentia (a.k.a. Morning Star)—*Fifteen-year-old daughter of Lakota warrior Wapitiyu Okle (Spotted Elk) and granddaughter to Chief Lone Horn. She's married to Isa.*

Jack O'Toole—*Father to Isa. Earned the Comanche name Pohya Isa, Walks With Wolves.*

Blue Flower—*Young sister to Spirit Talker and daughter to Buffalo Hump, she's married to Jack. They have four young children: George, Isa, Peter, and Nadua.*

George Freeman—*A Black cowboy who establishes a ranch on the North Platte River in Wyoming. Father to Esmeralda. Adopts Lakota child, Zebediah.*

Running Waters—*George Freeman's Pawnee wife.*

Esmeralda Freeman—*George's and Running Waters' ten-year-old daughter.*

Zebediah Freeman—*Foundling Lakota son of George and Running Waters.*

Juan Perez—*Creative, hard-nosed Mexican cook on Jack's trail drive.*

Taabe—*Wolf offspring of Zebediah. Mate to Mua.*

Tathanka (a.k.a. Buffalo Man)—*Oglala Lakota warrior who captures and befriends Isa O'Toole.*

Sergeant Blake Rawls—*Professional soldier assigned to keep an eye on Isa during the Yellowstone Expedition.*

Tatanka Wiiyaska (a.k.a. Buffalo Killer)—*Lakota warrior to whom Awentia is promised.*

Wapitiyu Okle (a.k.a. Spotted Elk)—*Miniconjou Lakota who is Morning Star's father.*

Hotamo'e (a.k.a. Bull Elk)—*A rogue Northern Cheyenne warrior.*

Will "Wally" Wallace—*Elderly mountain man still roaming the wilds of the frontier.*

Hap Cole and Dred Evans—*Cowboys on George Freeman's ranch.*

Burt Wilkins—*Horse breeding expert that Isa's father sends to help with the Quarter Horses.*

Lieutenant Wallace Dickerson—*An officer in General Crook's 2nd US Cavalry.*

Chester Donovan—*First hand hired on the Laramie Cross Breed Ranch.*

Historical Characters

William Tecumseh Sherman—*Famed Union general from the War Between the States, whom President Grant assigns to subdue the tribes of the Great Plains.*

Tasunke Witko (aka, Crazy Horse)—*Future chief of Oglala Lakota of the Sioux Nation.* He is *about 19 years old at the time of this story, but already gaining the attention of tribal leaders. He will go on to lead the massacre of General Custer's troops at Little Bighorn (aka, Greasy Grass) in 1876.*

Tatanka Iyotake (aka, Sitting Bull)—*Chief and medicine man of Hunkpapa band of Lakota Sioux.*

George Armstrong Custer—*Flamboyantly famous US Army officer and cavalry leader who performed valiantly in the War Between the States and early Indian Wars but is massacred at Little Bighorn.*

Red Cloud—*Highly regarded Chief of the Oglala Lakota nation who led the defeat of the US Army at the Fetterman Fight in 1866. His warriors also fought at Little Bighorn.*

Colonel David Stanley—*Commander of Fort Laramie in 1873 and leader of the Yellowstone Expedition to survey for the Northern Pacific Railroad.*

Dull Knife—*Northern Cheyenne chief and ally of Lakota chief Red Cloud.*

Little Wolf—*Northern Cheyenne chief and signatory to Fort Laramie Treaty of 1868.*

General George Crook—*Based out of Fort Laramie in 1876, his assignment was to eradicate the "Indian Problem."*

Isa's journey from Texas to the North Platte River country

The route used by Isa on his journey north from Texas as spawned from his vision quest. It featured challenging landscapes and many tribes known to be hostile.

The Frontier Calls: Two Souls, One Adventure

You are invited

Dear Reader,

Dear Reader,

A teen half-breed, a one-man pony, a warrior woman, and a wolf tame the 1870s frontier. That about sums up my story. If you're reading the Wolf Tales series, then it's likely that *Perilous Trails* and my pa's Frontier Chronicles series must have fully grabbed you. This second part of my tale begins in 1876, following my leaving home on a vision quest. I am sixteen-years-old but a grown man by frontier standards. Motivated by having had to kill a murderous Mexican *pistolero,* I left my family to embark on my own adventure of personal discovery.

The Frontier Calls: Two Spirits, One Adventure continues the testing of my courage, faith, endurance, pure grit, and search for a life mission. How I now share it with my warrior woman wife Morning Star. My folks named me Isa, which translates in Comanche to Wolf. I expect that I should add that my pa is White and my ma is a Comanche. That makes me, my brother Peter, and young sister Nadua what folks called half-breeds. As you'll find out, this can be a blessing and a heavy burden. Do keep in mind that my story incorporates history not found in most school history books. This book relates my tale as driven by fate and guided by God.

I have met up with plenty of Indians, especially Comanche and Lakota Sioux, so you'll find me using some of their language throughout *The Frontier Calls.* I have provided a handy glossary of Comanche and Lakota words toward the back of this book. I also provide a convenient glossary of frontier terms.

I'm a Christian, but I have tried to grasp the Comanche and Lakota cultures to better understand them. The Indian religion is based upon what is referred to as animism, in which every common natural item, from fish and animals to plants, trees, waterways, and mountains, were believed to have souls or spirits. The spirits and traditions connected with them guided the Comanche and Lakota. Their passion for their spirits no doubt gave them their fearlessness, as fed by the belief that they were protected in everything they did. Would they kill to defend their beliefs? Theirs was not a religion of love and forgiveness.

Could Indians like the Comanche or Lakota become Christians? My stories in the Wolf's Tales share my personal evolution at the intersection of faith and culture. It was like Saint Patrick's conversion of the Irish to Christianity, folding many of their less-offensive heathen rites into the Catholic faith. Would this work with the Indians? Well, it's part of the story.

As you follow my adventures, ask yourself whether you might be up to meeting the challenges I take on. Dangers? Privations? Hmmm. How might you have fared? Through it all, I first relied on the teachings from my family, then went on to learn from the raw and risky experiences I faced. I learned to trust in instincts forged from my biblical lessons.

To be straight here, I had no idea that my story was going to fill multiple volumes until I began to write it all down. I invite you to follow my adventures on America's western frontier.

Kindest Regards,
Isa "Wolf" O'Toole

Prologue

Just as I followed Morning Star through the doorway, an arrow buried itself in the wood beside my head. It was an attention-getter. I ducked into the cabin as a second arrow whizzed past my head and hit the far interior wall of the cabin.

Morning Star and I stared at it. "Cheyenne!" we said simultaneously.

"Hotamo'e kill!" came a not far-off cry.

I peeked out from the cabin window, and it drew another arrow from Bull Elk that thudded harmlessly into the window frame.

I sighted my Spencer through a gun port we'd had the wisdom to drill into the door. What I saw next was more than concerning. Four Cheyenne warriors stood beside Bull Elk. So, he had brought together his own band to join the rogue savage. I knew that Bull Elk's patience would quickly wear thin, as Indians generally did not like sieges, and he would be no exception. He strode to the top of the berm with his four companions. "Hotamo'e kill!" he shouted.

I reckoned it was time for action. I aimed the Spencer and squeezed off a shot. The blast about blew out our ears in the confined space of our cabin, but one of the Cheyenne caught my bullet in his arm and toppled back. I levered another round into the receiver and fired. I missed, but the Cheyenne dove back to cover. I figured they wouldn't be poking their heads above the berm again for a while.

"What we do?" asked Morning Star.

I shook my head. "We wait until dark," I responded. I had a trick up my sleeve unless Bull Elk did something unexpected before then. A part of me resented the Cheyenne's interruption of our wedded bliss.

We were in quite a fix. I wondered what had become of Taabe? What was on his wolf heart? With five hostiles out there, he was likely hesitant to attack.

Every now and then, Bull Elk sent an arrow at the cabin as a reminder of his presence.

Morning Star and I struggled patiently as we awaited darkness. There'd be no moon visible this night, so we might be able to escape.

What was on the mind of that rogue Cheyenne? Maybe they were also waiting for the night.

The sun soon completed its descent behind the mountain beyond our cabin. Darkness slowly enveloped the landscape, though we could still see a glow from Bull Elk's fire. The stars were mostly hidden behind clouds, thus adding to the virtual blackout.

We snuffed out the one candle in the cabin and plunged ourselves into total darkness. We'd now move about by feel. We waited while our eyes adjusted to the lack of light. Once outside, the partially hidden stars would offer us just enough light. We waited. When would he attack?

If Bull Elk was watching, the darkness in our cabin surely signaled to him that we were up to something. Turned out he was the one who acted first. He lofted a burning arrow into the cabin roof.

Chapter 1

Escape!

The cabin roof was dry and caught fire right quickly. There was no way we could get up there and snuff it out. We heard an arrow hit the front door.

At this hour, I doubted anyone from George's house would see the flames. My family had hung around for a couple of weeks before heading back to Texas. There'd be no patrols from Fort Laramie roaming about at night. Rescue didn't seem likely.

I reckoned we were surrounded. The Cheyenne hostiles were shouting and carrying on with taunts and threats in an attempt to make us come outside. In the near blackout, I sensed Morning Star's concerned *what next* look. Smoke began to seep into the cabin.

I groped along the floor in the darkness and pushed aside a buffalo skin rug along the far wall to reveal a hidden hatch. I could feel it, but couldn't see it. I managed to find the handle and pull it open with considerable effort.

Escape awaited us. I had just grasped Morning Star's arm to pull her toward me when I heard a buzz from the hole. A rattlesnake had made its home in the space under the floorboards and was none too happy about being disturbed. What to do? Cheyenne savages were hollering and waiting outside to kill us, the cabin was on fire, and our only avenue of escape was blocked by a venomous reptile.

We were desperate, and our situation grew more urgent by the second. I stood over the opening, aimed my Spencer into our escape hole, and began levering rounds and firing. With the noise outside and the crackling of the fire on the roof, the shots went virtually unnoticed by our attackers. Morning Star and I dared not get too close to the snake, but we listened intently. There was no rattle.

"We must go!" I whispered intensely, while saying a prayer in my mind that I'd killed the snake. Just in case, I swept the hole with the butt of my Spencer. I struck what I figured to be the rattlesnake's body. There was no response, so I lowered myself into the space. Morning Star hesitated for fear of the snake, but followed me.

The hole beneath the cabin offered a quick exit to a gully that ran past the privy and down to the North Platte River. Keeping our heads low, Morning Star and I squirmed along on our bellies. We heard a cry just to our left, *"Tanka! Tanka!"* Taabe and his pack had attacked one of the Cheyenne. We heard the thud of moccasin-shod feet running from our right. Realizing that the screams of his brother Cheyenne had ceased, the warrior paused at the chasm we were lying in. He happened to look down. Despite the darkness, there was enough starlight that he could see us.

"Hotamo'e!" he shouted as he nocked an arrow into his bowstring. His delay was costly.

Morning Star set her jaw and steeled herself. She

levered a round into the Henry, aimed best she could, and fired at the Cheyenne.

The bullet's impact sent the savage sprawling. Wounded, he regained his footing. Morning Star's bullet had split his bow in two and lodged in his shoulder. Just as he drew his knife, another bullet from my warrior wife staggered him. He plummeted into the crevasse we occupied, nearly landing on top of us.

By my count, only Bull Elk and two other Cheyenne remained. I feared that Bull Elk had heard this dead warrior's call and would come running. "Run!" I cried.

We both stood and made a dash for the riverbank. I could hear the crackling of flames eating wood behind us, and soon the shouts of Bull Elk and his remaining warriors trying to find us. We hoped he'd think we were being consumed by the flames. He'd find the bullet-riddled body of his brother savage, soon enough. I prayed that the darkness would delay that discovery.

I decided that heading for George's house was too far in the dark and too great a risk. If Bull Elk suspected we'd escaped, he'd likely suspect that's where we'd head and block our escape. We had little choice. Holding our rifles high, we swam across the river. Upon reaching the far side, we took stock of our situation. We had our rifles, my Colt revolver and Bowie knife, and the clothes on our backs. Everything else was being consumed in the fire. "Praise God we're not hurt," I blurted in a near whisper.

Morning Star smiled and snuggled against me for warmth. "We live," she said. "God good?" she asked.

I nodded and held her tightly.

We watched, heartbroken, as our possessions burned. We hid in the trees to await daylight. It made no sense to travel in the darkness. Besides, I wanted to see what Bull Elk would do.

* * *

As the first rays of the sun peeked over the eastern horizon, we were able to see the smoldering heap of cinder and ash that had briefly been our home. Bull Elk had just discovered the mostly eaten body of one warrior and that of the savage Morning Star had shot. He was uttering some sort of frustrating shouts to the skies and waving his arms. I suspected that he was directing his berating at us, for he'd found no charred bones among the cabin ruins. He was flanked by the two remaining warriors. With one of them wounded, the odds between us had been leveled a bit.

We were far from safe. Bull Elk would eventually find our trail. Also, the Cheyenne had ponies. Did I say ponies? What had become of Paint and Morning Star's mare? The corral was in disarray.

We prepared to head upriver, as the paths would be rockier and more difficult for Bull Elk to track us. As we were about to leave, Taabe appeared. He stared at me, and I sensed that he would go with us. I ruffled his mane. Mua and their two offspring joined us, but the greatest surprise was the appearance of Paint and the mare. They'd actually followed us across the river.

"We are blessed," I said to Morning Star.

"Blessed?" she asked.

"God has provided for us," I responded.

She nodded, as though she wasn't quite convinced. For her, it was more coincidences, as she hadn't yet fully grasped my faith.

I pulled her to me. We were still damp and chilled

from our river crossing. We kissed. "We must go," I said as I held her.

We mounted up and took a final look at the remains of our cabin and the frustrated Bull Elk's rantings, and headed west. There was no further looking back. My vision quest had resumed. Or, had it never paused?

* * *

How long might it be before Bull Elk discovered our trail? There was no way of knowing the depths of his depraved hatred for us. The Northern Cheyenne was a weakened tribe. They'd been pushed from the Black Hills by gold miners and were threatened by ever-increasing stealers on the Oregon Trail. The US Army outpost of Camp Robinson was established in 1874 and garrisoned by the 3rd Cavalry in response to the need for a military presence near the Red Cloud Indian Agency in northwest Nebraska. The elite Cheyenne warriors called dog soldiers were long gone, having been relegated to the dustbin of defeat. The US Army was concerned about an ongoing friendship between the Cheyenne Chief Dull Knife and Chief Red Cloud of the Lakota. The consequence was a blight on the Cheyenne as an organized force, resulting in rogue splinter bands like Bull Elk's.

We decided to put as much distance as possible between us and our burned-out cabin. We were blessed with a warm, dry day. Our clothes would soon be fully dried.

I figured that Bull Elk would expect us to follow the North Platte, so I headed us on a track a few miles to the southeast. We had no food, no money, and were short on ammunition, so I hoped we'd intersect with the Oregon

Trail and find useful leavings from settler wagons. By dumb luck, a small possibles bag had been caught on my gun belt. Thus, we had fire-starting materials.

I reckoned to head northward to the Yellowstone River. It was a long way, and we needed to find and make provisions as best we could.

We stopped within sight of the Oregon Trail to rest our horses. No wagon trains were in sight, so we sat side by side on a hilltop and managed to clean our weapons and take stock of what we had. Taabe and his pack rested close by. They'd alert us of any danger.

"Where we go?" asked Morning Star.

I placed a gentle hand on her shoulder. "North." I solemnly pointed northward.

She gave me a quizzical look. "No George? No Running Waters?"

"That's the first place Bull Elk will look for us. I don't want to place them in danger." My response was a mouthful of English for Morning Star to absorb, but she was learning my tongue quickly.

"Tathanka?" She posed the possibility of Crazy Horse's encampment.

I hadn't considered that. Crazy Horse and Buffalo Man had come to our wedding.

"They help," she advised. "Then, we go north?"

"We must first find what we can along the trail." I was hopeful of finding some tack for our mounts and maybe some discarded clothing.

"We find buffalo?" she suggested.

I cogitated on that. It was another great idea and would help if we could find one of the beasts. The buffalo was an essential ingredient to the Indian way of life. Every shred of a buffalo from hide to meat to bone had a practical purpose. I studied my new wife. I dared not underestimate her resourcefulness. I recalled Spotted Elk's tale of the bow and arrow and the importance of balance in our relationship. We each had strengths to contribute. "Let's see what we find and then go to Tathanka."

I expected a simple nod. Instead, she turned and had her way with me.

* * *

The Oregon Trail proved something less than satisfactory as a provider. Other than discarded furniture, occasional graves, and the bleached bones of livestock, there was nothing of value. I guess I shouldn't have been surprised.

"Let's go to Tasunke Witko and Tathanka," I finally admitted that Morning Star's suggestion had been the right course.

We crested a hill, and lo and behold, a small herd of buffalo confronted us. I pointed to a sizable cow within fifty feet of us. I readied my Spencer rifle.

"No," said Morning Star urgently.

I gave her a questioning look.

She pointed to a nearby ravine. It dropped off straight down for roughly a hundred feet. "Make buffalo go there," she said excitedly. "No shoot."

What Morning Star suggested made perfect sense. If we could chase the cow over the cliff, the fall would kill her and save us ammunition. I'd heard of Indians using such methods, driving entire herds of the beasts off cliffs with the result of provisioning their people for months. Having driven domestic livestock, I reckoned myself a tad more experienced than Morning Star. I used hand signals to illustrate how we'd approach from either side to place the buffalo cow between us and the ravine. Once in position, we'd wave our hands and shout to chase the cow over the cliff. There were no bulls or calves close at hand, so we looked to be in the clear.

Morning Star smiled. "Is good," she agreed.

We mounted up, snuck around behind the buffalo cow, and got ourselves in position. I made a final scan of our surroundings. There was still no sign of danger. To my surprise, Taabe and his pack came alongside. I figured the buffalo would be none-too-appreciative of wolves. Sure enough, the buffalo began to paw the ground nervously. I nodded to Morning Star, and we began shouting and waving our arms to scare the living daylights out of that cow. We even got Paint and the mare into riling that cow.

Well, the cow feinted as though wanting to join the rest of the herd, but she saw her escape path blocked. She turned and headed at an all-out run toward the cliff. If she realized the drop-off was ahead of her, it didn't matter. Her momentum carried her over the edge. We heard her land with a mighty thud and grunt followed by silence.

We headed off down the steep slope away to our side so as to safely reach the base of the ravine. Taabe arrived ahead of us. In his eagerness for a meal, he and the pack were putting the buffalo out of her misery. Obviously, he'd earned a share of our kill. That we could go in and begin to butcher the buffalo cow with no protest from the pack was a testament to our relationship.

The ravine turned out to be doubly convenient. In addition to providing us with the means of killing the buffalo, it offered shelter to build a cooking fire by which we could fill our empty stomachs.

We soon had a goodly selection of meat and even

skinned the buffalo. Skinning the buffalo with only my Bowie knife was no easy task, but we managed it. We soon were able to stand back to admire our efforts. We'd earned it. These were our first steps at being truly self-sufficient.

I built a small fire, and it wasn't long before we were chewing on the fruits of our labor. Of course, I did offer a blessing over our meal. We soon joined Taabe and the pack as fully sated. This having been said, I knew that we could not survive on buffalo meat alone. We'd have to balance our diet with fruits and vegetables. I recalled how the need for a balanced diet had turned my warring Comanche ancestors into nomadic traders ruling the Comancheria back in Texas.

I was pleased that Morning Star had suggested going to Crazy Horse's village. Hopefully, we could reprovision and head northward, as I was still of a mind to put distance between us and Bull Elk.

I fashioned a travois, using buffalo intestines to lash the poles together. With the mare pulling the travois and Morning Star and I riding Paint, we headed for the Oglala Lakota encampment. Taabe, Mua, and their now full-grown offspring followed us. I expect our caravan offered quite a sight to anyone spotting us.

* * *

It was with a mix of relief, gratitude, and hope that we approached the Oglala Lakota encampment at the headwaters of the North Platte River. Women washing clothing in the river were among the first to greet us. Blessedly, we were recognized. There were apprehensive gazes at Taabe and the pack, but we were able to peacefully enter the village and ride among the teepees on our way to offer our bounty to Crazy Horse. Most of those whom we passed offered welcoming smiles that turned uneasy at the sight of the wolves. For their part, Taabe and the pack paid no attention to the humans. Besides, their bellies were still full of buffalo.

It wasn't long before we found our self at Crazy Horse's teepee. I reached out and struck a drum hanging from a pole outside the entrance. It wasn't necessary.

Alerted by the noises of a gathering throng, the chief emerged. Upon seeing us, he offered a broad smile. "*Hau, mitákuye oyás'e,* Isa, Awentia," he said as a welcome. It occurred to me that White folks, especially, didn't realize that the fierce warrior chief had a warm heart.

"*Wowahwa, kola,* Tasunke Witko," I responded to his greeting with a wish for peace and friendship. We shook hands.

Buffalo Man heard of our arrival and joined the gathering. His gaze shifted between us and Crazy Horse. Our town and dirt-covered buckskins and absence of saddles for our horses were a clue of us being in desperate straits. "What happen?" he asked in halting English.

"Cheyenne *kize,* Tathanka," blurted Morning Star before I could respond.

"How many?" signed Crazy Horse.

I held up five fingers. "*Katá,*" I added, holding up two fingers to indicate that we'd killed two.

"Ínyan!" Morning Star signed how they'd burned our cabin, but we'd escaped.

"You lose everything?" signed Buffalo Man.

Morning Star and I looked at each other. I took her hand and then motioned to her and to the horses. "We have this," I said.

Buffalo Man spotted the burden on the makeshift travois.

"Bring gift for Tasunke Witko and Oglala Lakota," I offered. There was a goodly amount of buffalo meat remaining despite the wolves and us having eaten some of it. I think Buffalo Man was impressed with our resourcefulness at fashioning the travois. I hadn't yet told him how we'd killed the buffalo.

"Isa, Awentia, no *iyaya,*" invited Crazy Horse. "*Kola mato.*" He invited us and Buffalo Man to join him for a meal. He clearly yearned to learn more of our encounter with the Cheyenne. He was well aware of Red Cloud's friendship with the Cheyenne Chief Dull Knife. Crazy Horse opened the flap to his teepee and motioned us to enter.

At that, the gathered men and women left to attend to their daily tasks. I was about to enter the teepee, when a young boy approached Paint and the mare. He was bolled over for his trouble. We all laughed. My pinto was a one-man horse, and his steadfast loyalty carried to the mare. I signed that I must first see to the horses.

Crazy Horse nodded. The Indians of the plains fully appreciated the value of horses.

Morning Star and I led our horses to the river to wash away the dust of our travels. As I brushed Paint with a piece of juniper branch, I gazed out at the rolling hills. Somewhere, out there, a crazed Cheyenne was hunting us.

CHAPTER 2

NEW DIRECTIONS

We shared the full story of our battle with Bull Elk and his band. Crazy Horse and Buffalo Man were fully impressed with how we'd escaped and then survived. I fully credited Morning Star's resourcefulness with killing the buffalo. In fact, she sat with me rather than serving food with the other Lakota woman.

I think Crazy Horse and Buffalo Man were uncomfortable at first with my insisting on Morning Star's place at our meal, but they got over it. They likely chalked it up to White man's ways, given that I was half White. In fact, I invited Morning Star to sit with us because our spirits were now joined as one. You might say we were two spirits on one adventure.

It occurred to me that the encounter with Bull Elk, in combination with being sheltered in the Oglala Lakota village, might put the relationship between Red Cloud and Dull Knife in some jeopardy. No one had as yet brought the subject up, but I sensed that it hadn't missed Crazy Horse's consideration. He was far too wise and sensitive to tribal politics to miss the underlying difficulties.

Buffalo Man invited us to sleep in his teepee, but we gratefully declined. As Morning Star and I had already discussed, our aim was to resupply and leave as soon as possible. We felt the need to put distance between us and Bull Elk. Thus, we slept under the stars surrounded by our wolf companions.

The presence of Taabe and his pack was ignored by the prideful warriors but attracted cautious attention from children. Any time a child would come close, Taabe would curl his lips just enough to reveal fangs.

The generosity of the Oglala Lakota was a true blessing. It wasn't lost on me that Morning Star was being treated as a warrior. When Tathanka gifted me with a bow and arrows, he saw to it that Morning Star also received the same. Knowing the work that went into making the weapons, I found myself especially appreciative of the generosity and recognition.

The soft lavender of sunrise was painted across the eastern horizon. Sunlight peeked from behind a cloud in an otherwise cloudless sky. I stared for a few minutes at my beautiful, still-sleeping wife, stroked Taabe's mane, and stood to face the day. The encampment had not yet come to life as I eased over to Paint. I found that stroking his neck was soothing to my soul. A saddle lay beside him. Again, the generosity of the Lakota was beyond my wildest expectations. It wasn't like the fine leather saddles I'd become used to at my home back in Texas or the ones we'd lost to Bull Elk's attack. The Indian saddle was a far more-humble affair, but utilitarian nonetheless. I freed a parfleche bag that one of the Lakota warriors had tied to the saddle. It was heavier than I'd expected. The weight turned out to be for good reason. There must have been at least thirty .56 caliber cartridges for my Spencer carbine. We were indeed blessed. I cinched the bag and retied it to the saddle.

I thought on how the White man, especially the powerful men in Washington and the generals deciding Indian fates, hadn't a clue as to the true impact of their actions. The Fort Laramie Treaty of 1868, as hollow an agreement as it was, had been broken multiple times. The government seemed to continually fail at telling the tribes how to live their lives. Many Indian boys no longer had fathers to guide them, to instill the discipline of the warrior and culture of the tribe. Daughters became easy prey for renegades and bandits. Even in victory, there was defeat. Whether winner or loser, warriors returned to their camps to hear the wailing and chest beating of the women. The hordes of settlers far overwhelmed the ability of the tribes to replace lost warriors and mothers. Battle, disease, and a dwindling food supply were already beginning to take their toll. While some portrayed the Indian savages as noble peoples, they were actually frozen to ancient times.

As I stood, absentmindedly stroking Paint, a warm hand grasped my arm. "Good morning, Awentia," I said. Her hand was slender, soft, and loving, belying the warrior soul that flowed through her being. I turned and hugged my wife.

She kissed me. "We go soon?" She understood that we must move on.

I nodded. "We must."

She stared into my eyes as though searching into the very depths of my soul. "I love you." The words flowed gently from her lips. Then, she smiled and nudged me with her elbow. "Let's eat," she cooed with a motion toward Buffalo Man's teepee. Whatever Morning Star had seen with that penetrating gaze into my inner being must have delivered the answer she'd sought.

Here we stood at peace in a Lakota encampment that would have torn an enemy to shreds. Part of me stood in my pa's White world. With Morning Star, I was likely more Indian, but with the inclinations of my White lineage. The presence of Taabe served to more fully cement our attachment to the wilds of America's frontier.

Eat? I didn't have to be asked twice.

We headed for Buffalo Man's teepee.

We spent the next couple of hours talking in our mix of sign, English, Comanche, and Lakota. I had begun to realize that for the foreseeable future, Morning Star and I were warriors. Ours would not be the lives of my parents until much uncertainty was resolved. My vision quest would continue until the purpose and meaning of our lives were revealed. Only God knew what lay on our trail. Only He knew what would bring us contentment with life. Our morning repast ended with a round of pipe smoking. The men performed admirably at containing their mirth, as Morning Star choked several times on the smoke from the pipe. She gamely stayed the course and managed to enjoy one pass without coughing.

The generosity of the Lakota far exceeded expectations. I felt as though we were welcome to stay with them, but we all recognized that Morning Star and I were called to leave.

We spent the day taking stock of our provisions. I was especially concerned with our weapons. While hunting was a given, we'd likely also have to defend ourselves. I had the Spencer, Colt revolver, and Bowie knife we'd left our burning cabin with. Morning Star carried the Henry rifle. The quivers given to us by our Lakota friends contained both flint-tipped and steel-tipped arrows. Nearly all were exceptionally straight. Buffalo Man explained how he preferred the flint tips for battle, as they delivered the deadlier wounds more likely to end a fight. It made sense, as the deadlier the weapon, the greater the chances for survival. Buffalo Man believed that the whispered killing power of the arrow was more advantageous than the booming force of the rifle, with its betrayal of the shooter's location. I recognized that every weapon had its purpose and limits of effectiveness.

A tomahawk rounded out our weaponry. I hefted it. The balance seemed perfect. Like the knife, the tomahawk was a very personal fighting tool. It took both physical and mental strength to use it effectively.

We were offered a packhorse, but I was concerned that it would make stealthy travel more difficult. Also, three horses might be too tempting for any roving band of Indians to resist. We reckoned to travel away from regular trails; even avoiding game trails. We would make Bull Elk's hunt as difficult as possible. If possible, I aimed to eventually turn the tables on the rogue Cheyenne savage. Pa used to say that turning the hunter into the hunted should be a priority, whether pursuing beast or human.

* * *

A dry crisp morning with cloudless skies greeted us for our day of departure. We'd spent three days with the

Oglala Lakota with no sign of Bull Elk. Somewhere out in the vast wildness, he surely was hunting for us. He possessed far too much hatred and humiliation to give up his vendetta.

Our final expressions of gratitude to our hosts took at least an hour. They'd been exceedingly generous. Buffalo Man, having traveled with Crazy Horse around the Yellowstone River, counseled us extensively on water sources, landmarks, and places to avoid. We were warned about the Crow and Shoshone. The Crow, having served the enemy Whites as scouts, were more a concern of the Lakota. Crazy Horse gifted me with a beautiful pipe that he promised would serve me well, if indeed we encountered Sitting Bull.

We were soon mounted up and offered final farewells, as we pointed our horses northward. While the summer's warmth would soon be blanketing the wilderness, for now we could enjoy spring's colorful festival of rushing streams, lush green trees, and bright flowers. The Oregon Trail and the North Platte River were quickly left behind us.

It was for a time like this that my pa and ma had taught me about fending for food on the frontier. Coupled with all that Morning Star had learned as a young girl among her Miniconjou Lakota people, we were well-equipped to enjoy feasts as we traveled. In addition to plentiful game, there was a delicious abundance of wild spinach, acorns, and pine nuts aplenty, wildflowers, and berries—especially wild raspberries. In sum, our diet would be well-balanced. It was a must, as the frontier demanded alertness and considerable energy. All that was missing was coffee, though I hoped we would encounter traders or settlers who would trade for some. A Texan without coffee was a lost soul. Love for coffee must have been infectious, as Morning Star expressed her yearning for the tasty and aromatic liquid gold.

Our off-trail experience was an adventure unto itself. We traversed rocky outcroppings and dense forested areas. Late spring meant that grasses were particularly lush, much to the dietary enjoyment of our horses. In fact, I was concerned that they didn't overeat.

* * *

We were about midway through our third day of travel, when we rounded a bend in the trail to find ourselves face-to-face with a Crow hunting party of five warriors.

They must have been a tad bewildered to see a rather fierce-looking, tall young man and a Lakota woman decked out in buckskins and bristling with weapons. They had a decision to make.

I offered a peace sign to open communication. As I did so, I recognized one of the hunters as one of the Crow scouts I'd worked with on Colonel Stanley's Yellowstone Expedition. "Greetings, Climbing Bear," I ventured.

The former scout smiled as he recollected where he'd seen me. "Isa?" he asked.

The other four Crow appeared a bit disconcerted, for by now Taabe and his pack had appeared. Their eyes flitted from me to Morning Star to the wolves. "This Awentia." I introduced Morning Star with a hand sign that she was my wife.

The Crow nodded. They looked to be growing more comfortable with the situation.

I saw that they had three deer draped across a packhorse. Their hunting had apparently been successful. We had little food for sharing, but I figured to be sociable. "We rest." I pointed to a nearby stream.

We all dismounted and began watering our horses. I explained to Climbing Bear that a Cheyenne was hunting us. The Cheyenne were enemies of the Crow, so Climbing Bear promised he'd keep his eyes open for the rogue warrior.

As we sat, Climbing Bear suddenly turned serious. "I go to Fort Lincoln. Bloody Knife and Lean Bear scout for Yellow Hair. He go Black Hills with many soldiers."

I nodded. Was Climbing Bear inviting me?

The Crow hunter grew more concerned than serious. "Yellow Hair look for yellow rocks," he confided what he considered a dark secret.

We both knew that any discovery of gold led to breaking treaties, as miners flocked to the prospect of quick riches. I shook my head with dismay.

Morning Star gave me a questioning look.

"Isa no scout with Yellow Hair. Go to Yellowstone." I wanted there to be no mistaking our intentions. "Vision quest," I added the words that gave my words spiritual force.

Climbing Bear nodded his understanding. "Another time, my brother," he said evenly.

We were soon mounted up and headed our separate ways, us to the northwest and the Crow northeast toward Fort Abraham Lincoln. Once out of earshot, I tuned to Morning Star. "Whites come for gold. Much evil follows."

"Why God let bad happen?" she asked earnestly.

I sighed but understood her implication of why God didn't simply make everything right. "God gave us choices. We are free to decide. Some make good choices, some bad."

She shook her head resignedly.

* * *

This was big sky country. Well, the frontier could pretty much all be called big sky. Blueness stretched from horizon to horizon and beyond. We continued to avoid game trails. Ravines, hogbacks, and dense forest growth slowed us, but would challenge the tracking skills of the very best hunter. I doubted that Bull Elk would be up to the task.

The landscape was beautiful and often majestic. I watched an eagle soar high above and then dive for its prey. Tracks of what seemed to be every animal known to man abounded. Prints from mountain lion, bear, fox, deer, elk, coyote, and more were, investigated by Taabe and his pack. Surely, this was a place sanctified by God.

"Watch out!" I warned as I spotted a rattlesnake coiled on a nearby rock only ten feet away.

Morning Star's head swiveled to keep an eye on the reptile as we rode on by.

As the day wore to an end, we rode to the top of a low rimrock to scan our backtrail. Gazing back at the hills and crevices we'd traversed, there was no sign of anyone following us. Dared we think that Bull Elk had given up the chase? We descended to a place under the rock outcropping. It afforded us shelter, while the tops of junipers shielded us from view. Coals from a fire lay in the middle of this natural refuge, but it had burned many moons back. There was a flat area shielded by bushes to one side; a perfect spot for our horses. We decided to chance a fire, both for cooking and warmth. It was nearly summer, but there was still snow on the highest peaks.

Here we were journeying on my vision quest; a quest that had apparently become ours. Only God knew what adventure lay ahead. There was a romance to it, and my warrior woman was very much up to romance. No words were spoken. We were soon focused on just the two of us. We'd escaped a burning cabin surrounded by murderous savages, received much-needed help from our Lakota brothers and sisters, and now, we were on the trail to wherever. We'd enjoy this night in our mountain sanctuary.

Chapter 3

Surprise Discovery

We necessarily dressed quickly in the chill morning air. The remaining embers from our cooking fire were woefully insufficient to warm us. Morning Star stirred the coals to no avail. I sure wished we had some coffee. Watching her, I deeply appreciated her beauty.

She must have felt my eyes upon her as she turned with a winsome expression. She sighed. "Must go?" she asked unconvincingly. We could have spent the day here in our hideaway.

I sighed. "Yes, we must go."

With the horses saddled and packed, we led them on foot along a gentle slope through junipers and then aspen. We mounted up and rode easy-like beside the waters of a gurgling, crystal-clear creek. Rounding a bend in the stream, I spotted wisps of smoke rising perhaps a mile away.

We reined in and dismounted. The horses enjoyed the respite as they drank their fill. We hadn't seen a human since the encounter with the Crow hunting party, and the smoke aroused my innate curiosity.

"Shall we?" I asked with a head nod toward the distant sign.

I had just squatted to drink when I saw Morning Star's eyes grow wide with surprise. I pivoted and stood to face what could best be called a throwback creature. It was a man; make no mistake about that. He was at least my height and thirty pounds heavier. Under a floppy leather hat, he wore a thick gray beard that barely hid the crevasses indelibly carved into his face by nature's elements. The long hair framed sparkling blue eyes. His fringed buckskins were soiled with the sweat, blood, grease, and grit of many years in the mountains. He hefted an ancient flintlock rifle, and a large knife hung from a red sash wrapped around his waist. My mouth gaped.

"Wahg! Y'all headed fer the vous?" The gravelly sound spewed from his near-toothless smile.

We were instantly disarmed by the man's presence. "Vous?" I asked.

"The great gatherin'. Happens ev'ry year up at the 'Stone," he stated. The man's English was leaving something to be desired. "Name's Will Wallace, but y'all kin call me Wally."

"I'm Isa O'Toole. This is my wife, Awentia," I said and returned the introduction.

"Isa?" questioned the old man. "Thet be wolf in Comanch," he observed. "And she be Morning Star; a fetchin' beauty, I must say. Lakota...Miniconjou?"

I was at a loss for words and simply nodded.

"Come join me yonder," he invited. "Got some coffee brewin'," he said with a twinkle in his eye.

As we silently followed Wally to his campsite, it wasn't lost on me that he'd caught us totally unawares. It could as easily have been Bull Elk sneaking up on us.

Aside from the small cooking fire with a blackened coffee pot set atop it, we quickly noted an old horse and a pack mule. A small stack of pelts was surrounded by a half dozen traps. "Much beaver?" I ventured with a nod toward the pelts.

"Big outfits done over-trapped," Wally lamented. He looked from me to Morning Star. "Y'all fetch yer cups an' set a spell," he invited.

I retrieved our cups from our gear and rejoined the camp.

Wally's big, gnarly hands grasped the hot handle of the coffee pot with nary a wince, and he filled our cups.

Dang, but it was about the best coffee that had ever passed my lips. "Thanks kindly, Wally."

"See yuh be a man of faith," he noted with an eye to my bear claw necklace with its cross. "Where you young folks headed?" he asked.

"Yellowstone," replied Morning Star. Her eyes grew with intensity as she revealed her own necklace with its cross. "God good."

"She speak good 'lish," complimented Wally.

Morning Star smiled in response.

"Who be chasin' yuh?" said Wally with a knowing expression on his craggy face.

How did he know? I gazed thoughtfully at the man. He was stuck in some long past time, but wise, observant, and seemingly kind. "Northern Cheyenne," I stated matter-of-factly.

"Dog soldiers be long gone," Wally observed. "Dull Knife band?"

"No. He's a renegade named Hotomao'e. Makes plenty trouble," I replied.

Wally nodded. "Ne'er heard of him." He shifted the

coffee pot hanging over the fire. "Yuh know Tatanka Iyotake be ahead." Wally was warning us of Sitting Bull.

I smiled. "Tasunke Witko is a friend," I said.

"That be good, cuz y'all not wanna lose yer hair." He was obviously concerned.

I shifted the subject. "Where's this vous?"

"Four moons," he said with a wave of a paw. "Be up neah the 'Stone." Wally said this with a sense of longing.

I realized that Wally's *'Stone* was the Yellowstone River, but also sensed that his vous was a rendezvous. There was no longer the great gatherings of mountain men. I recalled George telling me of how the famed mountain man Jim Bridger had regaled visitors at Fort Laramie with exaggerated tales of his exploits. "Coffee's good," I said.

"Yer welcome to stay a spell," invited Wally.

The coffee alone made the invitation tempting, but I felt compelled to move on. If Bull Elk was trying to find us in this vast wilderness, I didn't want to put Wally at risk. It was likely a slim chance, but a chance, nonetheless. Morning Star and I exchanged a knowing look. It amazed me how well we could communicate without words. She was very much my soulmate. "Thanks kindly, Wally, but we must move on."

"Up to y'all. Invite always stands," he responded with a tinge of disappointment in his gravelly voice. He appeared to crave company while loving being alone. It was the deep inner conflict within most every mountain man. "Here, enjoy this." He handed me a small bag of coffee beans.

The aroma from the little bag was like some elixir of life itself. "Mighty obliged, Wally," I said gratefully.

Chapter 4

Shoshone!

I reckoned our path would keep us clear of Sitting Bull, and assuming he was on our trail, well ahead of Bull Elk. The landscape was often breathtaking in its rugged beauty. This was God's country, if ever such a place was to be so worthy.

We didn't want for food, as God's generous bounty lay around us. Here we were, two young travelers making our way to some unknown destination. My vision quest was now ours, as Morning Star was my companion, partner, and soulmate in the venture. I felt as though the quest had taken on a life of its own, and my Creator was taking us to some gloriously purposeful end. I hadn't a clue, though I had begun to yearn for it. George said that man plans while God laughs at those plans. No matter, as I had no plan—no destination—as yet.

Taabe still followed us, though it was apparent that his pack would soon grow. I wondered what it was about us O'Tooles that God had seen fit to partner us with wolves. And these weren't any old wolves. Like my pa's wolf Zeb, Taabe was as gentle with Morning Star and me as most any domestic dog.

After having skirted a large rock outcropping that took us into a creek-fed ravine, we decided to rest. Paint and the mare surely needed rest in the rarefied mountain air, and they were our most valuable assets. I looked up to see dark clouds gathering, presaging a storm. "We find shelter," I advised. We surely didn't want to find ourselves at the bottom of some ravine in a heavy downpour, as deadly flash flooding was a possibility. Many frontier travelers had underestimated the force of the onrushing water that characterized a flash flood and paid for it with their lives.

Morning Star pointed to a place above us. We scrambled up the steep slope toward it. The shelter was deep, as though a huge hand had scooped a place from the rock. It was a struggle to reach it, but we were all able to fit within its sheltering walls. We huddled together to watch in awe at the violent tempest descending upon us.

A bolt of lightning streaked from on high, followed by an ear-splitting peal of thunder, as though the sky had burst open. Rain began to gush down in torrents. In mere minutes, the little creek we'd quenched our thirsts in but a few minutes before had risen to little more than five or six feet from our shelter. The current was wild and quite deadly, as tree limbs careened past. Had we remained down in the ravine, we'd likely have been swept to our deaths. Lightning and thunder added to the theater of violence. The deluge lasted no more than half an hour. The receding waters soon revealed a wasteland.

The slope to the bottom was too slippery to navigate, so we decided to spend the night in our hillside shelter.

Water was plentiful, as enough pooled toward the rear of our sanctuary to satisfy us and our entourage. I built a small fire, splitting sticks to get at the dry wood inside. After eating, I lay back with Morning Star nestled in my arms and the wolves huddled around us like fur blankets against the post-storm chill.

We awakened hours later to the peeping of tiny wolf pups. The three newborns were nursing at Mua when they weren't playfully tumbling over each other. The proud papa stood by guarding his brood. His pack was growing.

The lavender glow of the sunrise sent warming shards of sunlight that would soon dry the slope below us sufficiently for us to climb down and resume our travels. As we gathered our personal effects and prepared to depart, Morning Star grabbed my arm and cupped her other hand to her ear. I heard it, too. I cautiously peered down from our hideaway to see about a dozen Indians trekking along the ravine. They were apparently gathering animals that had drowned in the flood. They were of a tribe neither of us was familiar with. We decided to lay low and wait for them to pass.

Leave it to Paint to decide to whinny. He was tired of being cooped up.

* * *

The hunters had nearly passed. It was the brave at the end of the hunting party who heard Paint. He stopped.

I placed my hand over Paint's snout to quiet him, but he snorted.

The hunter looked up and spotted our shelter. He called to the others, apparently telling them that he'd heard a horse up above them.

The other hunters laughed. What would a horse be doing up there?

The last brave was insistent. He was determined to investigate. He dismounted with the intention of climbing the slope to our hideaway. The others kept riding on.

The slope was still a tad slippery, and the brave had slung his bow over his shoulder. He obviously expected no threat.

I drew my Bowie knife.

As his head popped into view just above the edge of our shelter, I reached out and grabbed his hair and lifted him up while thrusting my knife to within inches of his face. I held him at arm's length with his feet dangling in the air.

His eyes grew wide with surprise. He was about to holler, but my threatening gaze dissuaded him of that. Still gripping his hair and with my knife now at his throat, I helped him climb the final steps into our shelter.

He was barely as tall as Morning Star but had a wiry build with sinewy muscles. As he gained his footing, he reached for his own knife. The metallic sound of a lever action broke the tension. Morning Star's Henry rifle aimed at his head disadvised him of pulling his knife.

I put my finger to my lips to caution silence.

By now, his companions had become curious as to where he'd disappeared to and began to double back.

I disarmed him and motioned him to sit. He was reluctant at first but obliged upon seeing Taaba and the pack. I reckon no Indian in his right mind would take on the sort of strong medicine implied by me and Morning Star traveling with wolves. "Isa," I said, pointing to my chest. "Comanche," I added, then pointed to Morning Star. "Awentia, Miniconjou Lakota." At the mention of

Lakota, the hunter's eyes widened with recognition, and he nodded vigorously.

We heard voices from below, so time was of the essence.

"Shoshone," said our captive with a hand motion to his chest.

If the hunters below decided to fight, we held a far superior defensive position, though they could climb the hill opposite us and make trouble. I made a peace sign to our Shoshone captive.

"Shoshone far from hunting grounds," said Morning Star. It seemed that this hunting party of Eastern Shoshone had traveled far beyond the tribe's normal territory far to our west. Somewhere not too far away would likely be a small temporary encampment, as they would not leave their families too far behind. I wondered what had driven them such a distance?

"Wirasuap," said our captive with a finger to his chest. He made a sign of a bear spirit.

So, his name was Bear Spirit. "Wirasuap…Isa," I said pointing from him to me. At least, we now knew names. It would help toward figuring a way out of any possible threat. I didn't sense that they were of a warring mind-set, but hunters could quickly change to warriors out here in the Wyoming wilds.

I took a look down into the ravine to see a half dozen arrows nocked in Shoshone bowstrings. I motioned Bear Spirit to me and had him lean out, so his companions could see him.

Bear Spirit spoke rapidly in Shoshone to his companions. To his credit, whatever Bear Spirit said to his fellow hunters caused them to put away their arrows.

"Ana o'a hi'it," I invited in Comanche while moving my closed fingers to my mouth in an eating motion.

Morning Star gave a small laugh at my attempt to open communications with the band. *"NiyáŋkA,"* she invited in the Lakota tongue.

Bear Spirit nodded, smiled, and pointed to a good-sized dry place along the south bank of the now-receded creek that offered plenty of space to accommodate all of us.

As the Shoshone party rode to the chosen spot, we made our way down the steep slope and followed. Taabe stayed behind. I sensed that he'd be staying here for a while with the newborn pups. Taabe parked himself on the edge of the shelter, where he could watch over our parley with the Shoshone.

We soon had a cooking fire aflame and were roasting venison steaks on a spit. Hands flew about mixed with grunts, facial expressions, drawings in the damp soil, and the four languages represented in the gathering.

Because he initiated our encounter, Bear Spirit spoke on behalf of the Shoshone. He described a place to the northwest of us that he said was filled with strong spirits. He described hot water spouting from the ground, big waterfalls, ponds with all manner of colors, hot springs, and a myriad of wonders that challenged the mind's eye. It was clear that the Shoshone had passed near this place and seen enough to be fearful of it. Bear Spirit noted that the Shoshone had signed a treaty giving them permission to hunt in the magical place he'd described. I recalled that George had referred to the place a time or two. Apparently, a couple of years back in '72, President Grant had signed a law establishing Yellowstone National Park with the aim of protecting its wonders from vandals and opportunists.

Mine and Morning Star's eyes lit up at the thought of exploring this wondrous place. We held none of the fears, nor superstitions shared by the Shoshone. Perhaps, we were just a tad foolhardy, if not overly adventurous.

With our meal ended, the Shoshone indicated that they intended to head westward toward their traditional hunting grounds. We said our goodbyes.

Morning Star and I spoke for a moment with our eyes. We knew where the vision quest was taking us. Perhaps the meeting with the Shoshone had been more than a coincidence. The time we had spent with the hunting party turned out to be of great value. It had come to me that time well spent was an investment in the future. Time was best redeemed by making the most of it, otherwise it was a waste. My thinking was that God gave us time on earth to make the best use of time. My pa often referred to a verse in Genesis about making the most of the bounty given us by God. He said it was God's command to do so.

We saddled the horses and prepared to resume our journey. I looked up to the hideaway and saw Taabe still watching us. The expression on his furry face said he'd catch up with us. It was as though he was assuring us that he'd be there when needed.

The experience with the Shoshone having ranged far beyond their traditional hunting grounds got me thinking how life was being disrupted by the wave of settlers heading west. There'd been a time when there were far more buffalo. The herds were shrinking along with the Indian way of life. I recalled how my uncle Spirit Talker and the Penateka Comanche had been shuttled off to a place up in the Indian Territory that folks called Oklahoma. I sensed that the disruptions would eventually lead to some sort of armed resistance. The question was when and where? I recalled Buffalo Man hinting at Crazy Horse allying with Sitting Bull to gather the tribes, sometime in the near future. When I was on the Yellowstone Expedition under Lieutenant Colonel Custer, the officer the tribes called Yellow Hair, there were rumors of General Sherman being under orders to eliminate what some called the Indian problem.

Chapter 5

Nature's Wonder

Morning Star and I nestled together before the dying flames of our small cooking fire. I looked off at the moon and stars. "Our way is ending," I said, with a heavy heart. This was the Comanche part of me speaking.

"Our people still tell the stories," she said in response to my heavy observation. "There is the wisdom of the mountains and waters, and there are songs in the trees. We are still of this earth and carry its message."

I looked into her eyes and kissed her. Her eyes came to life. She held much wisdom.

"God make all good," she added.

This was the first time Morning Star had been so forthright in attributing the creation to God. "Yes, yes. He did," I agreed.

We laid there taking in the quiet of the night. I recalled my ma telling me how she shared quiet times with my pa. With a faraway gaze, she would say it was often so quiet they could hear the stars twinkle. Just then, a coyote's howl broke the stillness of the night. Coyote? While I dared not compare a coyote to a wolf, the howl gave me pause to wonder how Taabe was getting on with his pack.

"Taabe good," said Morning Star.

How did she know what I was thinking? "How?"

"Eyes speak," she replied and kissed me. In but another moment, she was asleep.

My eyes fell to her as moonbeams caressed her gently beautiful face.

* * *

The terrain had become ever more rugged. We followed game trails, as breaking our own path had become tiresome and too slow. If Bull Elk was following, delay on our part was to his advantage.

We were driven by a burning desire to see this magical place so vividly described by the Shoshone. From their description, it would be hard to miss. Was it truly a place where spirits dwelled?

We had forded several rivers, the most recent having been what the Lakota called the Greasy Grass. Whites named it the Little Bighorn. Now, we stood on the south bank of the Shoshone River. Even in July, the distant mountaintops of the Absaroka Range were capped with snow. The effort of climbing caused a burning in our lungs, as the air seemed thinner. Trees and flowers bore testament to God's sense of beauty, but the mountains were stunningly grand. Big horn sheep and elk roamed freely. We kept a wary lookout for the hunters, as mountain lion, bear, bobcat, and wolf prowled for their meals. Beaver were still busy building dams, while squirrels, prairie dogs, and rabbits scurried about performing seemingly endless doings. Every turn of the trail brought an awe-inspiring vista.

Morning Star and I talked about whether we might have been so bold as to undertake this adventure had Bull Elk not burned us out of our cabin. Would we still be lazing about, dreaming of what we were now doing? We had turned a horrible circumstance into a new beginning.

We wondered, too, what George and Running Waters might be thinking of our long absence after the cabin destruction. We counted on Buffalo Man delivering our message to them.

* * *

It had been about ten days since our encounter with the Shoshone hunting party. They had told us of a pass at the headwaters of the North Fork of the Shoshone River. It took us north of the Absaroka Range. We were leading Paint and the mare up an inclined game trail, when we rounded a bend and came upon a sight that stole our breath. Words were fully inadequate to describe what lay before us. A huge lake lay before us, its waters sparkling like jewels beneath the afternoon sun. God had outdone Himself.

We felt exhilarated and picked up our pace.

The sun was creeping toward the horizon as we reached a piece of high ground overlooking the lake. We decided to make camp with this inspiring view of the lake before us. During a conversation while on the Yellowstone Expedition, Sergeant Rawls had told me that he'd heard of a large body of water called Yellowstone Lake at the headwaters of the river. I reckoned this had to be it. I figured that we were roughly a half mile from the shore of the lake. Rawls spoke admiringly of

President Grant having signed the legislation establishing the park.

"My people talk of this place," said Morning Star.

"What do they say?" I responded curiously.

"Strong medicine, Isa's *sunipu*. Many spirits," she explained. "They all live here."

I absorbed Morning Star's words. It seemed unsurprising that the tribes would revere this place. Their worship of many gods suited this environment. "Which way we go?" I asked. It was clear that we would not be heading due west without a boat.

Morning Star smiled and pointed to the northwest. "We follow big water."

"Big water is called Yellowstone Lake. We call a place of big water a lake," I gently informed her.

"We follow lake," she stated.

I had to admit that my beloved Texas Hill Country paled in comparison to the majestic vistas surrounding us. Then again and from what I'd heard, I wasn't inclined to spend a winter up in these parts. As these thoughts ran through my head, I gazed out toward the far-off shore. There were a half dozen grizzlies fishing in the water. Even at a distance, one seemed unusually big. I'd have bet he'd be at least ten feet tall standing on his hind legs.

I'd bagged a rabbit earlier in the day, so we built a small cooking fire and dined on the little fellow. I even managed to brew a couple of cups of coffee, remembering to bless our mountain man acquaintance.

"Coffee deli…" ventured Morning Star.

"Delicious," I said.

"Yes…that," she said with a laugh.

I loved her laugh, as it brought her face to life. I laid out our bedrolls. We let the horses graze freely. There was no point in staking them and leaving them vulnerable to predators. I considered keeping the fire stoked, but decided to let it die out. Paint would give plenty of warning of any threat. I took a final scan of the area, crawled into our bedroll, and nestled with Morning Star.

* * *

I awakened to a lavender glow painted across the eastern horizon. With the mountains casting their shadows, it'd be a couple of hours before the warming rays of sunlight graced our campsite. I looked beside me at my still-sleeping wife. I was blessed to have found such a strong life companion.

I apparently wasn't the only one who thought so. A pair of yellow eyes stared at me from across the clearing. The lion was perhaps forty feet away. A couple of leaps would put him in our laps. He sat there, tail twitching and eyes sizing us up. I wondered whether he realized the claws on my necklace came from one of his relatives.

I nudged Morning Star while slowly placing my hand over her mouth. A sudden sound or movement could set undesirable actions in motion. Ever-so-gently, I gripped the Spencer carbine with my free hand.

I hadn't yet figured why the big cat just sat there. I brought the Spencer into firing position. If the mountain lion decided to attack, I reckoned to get a couple of shots off before he could cover the ground between us. Why hadn't he moved?

A low growl behind me answered my question. I chanced a careful glance in my peripheral vision. Taabe!

I sat up. Mua and the rest of the pack, including the three pups, were with Taabe. The situation had become a standoff.

Morning Star was startled at the sight of the mountain lion but remained silent as the scene played out.

Slowly...ever-so-slowly, the big cat began to back off. He rightly figured that four full-grown wolves weren't worth fighting simply to dine on a meal of human flesh. Of course, he had no idea what a .56 caliber slug from my Spencer carbine would do to him. It didn't take long for the big cat to be loping away.

Taabe led his pack into our camp, and we enjoyed a happy reunion. Even at my size, playful wrestling with wolves is an exercise not to be taken lightly. The pups especially didn't yet understand that humans lacked the thick fur to protect against the biting of mock fighting. Taabe did his best to scold and instruct the youngsters.

* * *

There was an extra sense of security with the presence of the wolf pack, but we dared not let our guard down.

"What of Hotamo'e?" asked Morning Star, as we packed our gear for a day of exploring the land before us.

I sensed that Bull Elk was too filled with hatred to easily give up on hunting us. "We must watch our back trail," I said. It wouldn't be right to sugarcoat the threat we still faced. Morning Star would likely see right through me not being truthful about the danger.

Morning Star sighed and nodded. "Hotamo'e is coward," she concluded.

"But a dangerous coward," I said. "Let's go."

We were soon heading in a northwesterly direction following the shoreline of the vast body of water that we figured to be Yellowstone Lake. We ultimately aimed to skirt around the northernmost reaches of the lake, as the Shoshone had told of incredible sights. I gathered that these must have been the places that gave the region to the mystical and spiritual beliefs of the Indians. We were making great progress, alternately walking and riding Paint and the mare, when I felt a tingling sensation. A threat lurked nearby.

"Do you feel it?" I whispered to Morning Star as we rode side by side.

She nodded.

We both slowly scanned our surroundings as we rode. It occurred to me that we'd been doing a terrible job of hiding our trail. Hopefully, we weren't about to face a freshly reinforced Bull Elk war party.

"There's a stand of cottonwoods over yonder. Let's head there," I said with guarded urgency. There was a cluster of trees on slightly higher ground. It would also serve strategically as a good defensive position.

We nudged our horses to a canter and were among the cottonwoods within a couple of minutes. We dismounted to survey the area from the semi-hidden vantage point. We'd both grabbed our carbines as a precaution.

We didn't have long to wait.

Ambling along down the trail, sitting atop his mule was none other than Will Wallace. He stopped every now and then to examine the trail before him. Eventually, he arrived at the spot where we'd headed to the cottonwoods.

"Wagh!" he shouted. "I knows yer up thar!"

Morning Star and I shook our heads and smiled at each other. "Very dangerous," she said with a little laugh at our unfounded fears.

"Wally!" I called back to him. "You been following us all this time?"

He dismounted from his mule. With hands on hips

and feet spread, he responded with a hearty laugh. "By chance, my friends. Pure chance…until the past day. Saw yer wolf friends." Another great laugh escaped him. "Come on down. We make camp soon," he announced.

We noticed that he had a second mule we hadn't seen at our first meeting. We were on the run from Bull Elk and apparently hadn't noticed. It made sense that Wally would have a pack animal. Importantly, a freshly-killed buck lay across the pack mule's back. How Wally had managed that without us having heard gunfire puzzled me.

We led our horses down from the cottonwoods and greeted Wally with hugs.

"Whar yuh headed?" he asked.

"Shoshone told us of many places to the west. They said spirits lived there." I kept a serious expression in spite of Wally's knowing smile as I spewed out the words.

"Humph! I saw yer Shoshone. Friendly bunch," he noted. "Weren't goin' hungry fer sure."

"Reckon we have a couple of hours of good light ahead. You're welcome to join us," I offered.

"How were them Shoshones?" Wally asked, knowing there were at least ten in the hunting party.

Morning Star smiled. "Isa make Shoshone friendly," she replied in halting English. "Eat much elk."

"Yuv got yerself quite a woman thar, Isa," observed Wally.

"It took both of us to tame them," I assured him. Morning Star appreciated the acknowledgment of her contribution. "Tell you more over the campfire later." I took a long, appraising gander at Wally. He sure enough was old. He was a grown man back in the 1830s, so a little mathematics told me he was easily seventy years old. The weatherbeaten skin and deep crevices in his face bore testament to his many years in the wilderness fending for himself.

We stopped to take a breather and water our horses and mules.

"Hear tell guvmint folks be worried 'bout protectin' this place," he lamented.

I could appreciate his sentiments. What we'd seen thus far sure deserved protecting. "The government always seems to get its way, Wally," I ventured.

Morning Star glanced over at me appreciatively.

"Sure would be a crime to spoil it," I added. I recalled one of the Bible verses my pa had us memorize. "In the first chapter of Genesis, verse twenty-eight, in the Bible, God commands mankind to be fruitful, multiply, fill the earth, and subdue it. He doesn't say destroy it."

"I'd sure nuf keep that in yer thinkin', Isa." Wally nudged the mules along a bit faster to move ahead of us. He seemed to have something in mind.

We journeyed onward with little or no conversation until we reached a spot where a sparkling creek fed into the lake. The place had apparently hosted folks before, as there was plenty of evidence. Long-dead campfires and horse-trodden ground offered plentiful signs. Wally gave us a satisfied smile, as though this was a spot he was looking for.

Being as experienced in camping as we all were, we efficiently cared for the horses and mules and had a cooking fire going in no time. Wally did some deft butchering of the deer and soon had venison steaks roasting on a spit over the flames. Importantly, he broke out his trusty coffee pot.

As we watched the meat roast, I couldn't hold back

any longer. "How'd you kill the deer? We'd heard no gunshot.

That brought another of Wally's hearty laughs. "Din't waste a bullet. Got him with my knife," he said. With that, he demonstrated his talent with a knife, as he slipped it from its scabbard and threw its steely tip into a nearby cottonwood. "I be good fer 'bout thirty feet. Gotta get close to my prey."

"I'd like to throw like that," I said.

"Yuh need a knife with balance, Isa," he advised. He retrieved his knife from the tree and handed it to me. "Traded fer it with a Frenchie from up north," he noted. "It was from a place called Your Rope. Strange name fer a place."

I knew from my pa's teaching that he was referring to a place back east across a great sea that was called Europe and lay beyond a huge body of water called an ocean. Apparently, the ocean put this Yellowstone Lake to shame. I hefted the blade. As to balance, it put my Bowie knife to shame.

"Thing works fer self-defense, too," noted Wally. "No offense, but an Injun or two has felt its edge."

I passed the knife to Morning Star. She tested the balance, then, quicker than greased lightning, she threw it with deadly accuracy into the trunk of a cottonwood about a dozen feet away. Most men couldn't have matched her skill. "Good knife," she said with a knowing smile.

We sat back to enjoy venison with sides of wild spinach and berries, washing it all down with Wally's precious coffee.

* * *

Unbeknown to us, Bull Elk had reinforced his band and returned to his pursuit of Morning Star and me.

He had departed the Northern Cheyenne village, having disrespected Dull Knife's wishes to stay home and help defend the tribe. He'd persuaded two young hotheaded warriors impatient for battle to join him, and the two warriors already loyal to him. Dull Knife feared that pursuit of us would damage relations with the Lakota. It was about politics, not about us.

Bull Elk had a hunch that we were headed westward to the mystical place the Whites called Yellowstone. He skirted the Lakota villages, especially the Miniconjou and Oglala, and eventually encountered the Shoshone hunting party we had met. He was of a fighting spirit but saw no point in attacking a party that had him outnumbered. He was well aware that the Shoshone were fierce warriors. Bull Elk did learn from the Shoshone that we had passed through. It served to confirm that he was on our trail.

Bull Elk was a great hunter, so it didn't take him long to pick up the trail we were on. Of course, we had done little to disguise our path. There were plenty of sign to follow.

* * *

We shared with Wally our concern about Bull Elk and how he'd burned us from our cabin. Up to now, we had been in no particular hurry. If Bull Elk was indeed following us, we were confident that he'd be days behind. Now, my intuition kicked in, and I had a sense that he was closer than we dared think. I reckoned it was time to begin covering our backtrail. There was no point in making us any easier to track. With three of us, two horses, two mules, and a pack of wolves, covering our tracks was a challenge, if not impossible. Even hiding our trail by riding in streams was an ineffective tactic.

Wally was fully appreciative of our concerns. "How 'bout ole Wally here fall back an' keep an eye on yer backtrail?"

"We can't ask you to risk it, Wally," I replied.

"Dang, y'all! I'm an ole codger lookin' fer some 'citement. It be fun," he insisted. With that, he slowed. He let us get well ahead of him before turning away from the lake and keeping out of sight among the cottonwoods, spruce, and pine.

* * *

If Bull Elk was as good a track as he was thought to be, he sure was taking his sweet time catching up to us. While I had a feeling that he was drawing closer, I reckoned he'd still be at least a day or more behind us. Meanwhile, we trekked onward.

We were now about five days north from where we'd first spotted Yellowstone Lake. We followed the river north for about a day. We were of a mind to take a turn westward toward where the Shoshone had described incredible sights. We were about ready to make that turn to the west, when Wally urged us to ride along the river for just another hour.

Lo and behold, we were soon greeted by another incredible sight. It was a rancorous boiling cauldron. Its bubbly and turbulent sulfurous waters smelled like rotten eggs. It stretched out for quite a space before us, bathed in colors from yellow to a deep azure blue. It seemed alive with its seething spring waters and rising puffs of steam.

Wally smiled. He'd been here before and rightly figured it would impress us. "Now, we can head west," he advised, but with a grin that said there'd be plenty more.

"No wonder the Indians think this place holds magic," I observed, my eyes still taking in the wonder of the roiling waters.

"Strong *sunipu,*" remarked Morning Star.

"Y'all ain't seen nothin' yet," said Wally with deeply held confidence.

Having soon had our fill of the beautiful but smelly spring waters and in need of fresh air, we managed to cross the Yellowstone River. It lay wide in its meandering path before us. Despite it being late July, snow still capped the distant mountains.

We set up camp on the western shore. We'd exhausted Wally's supply of venison. This time, it was Morning Star whose arrow and unerring aim contributed to our feast. She put an arrow through a pike that had been swimming lazily near the riverbank. Fish was a nice break from venison and elk and rabbit. Taabe wasn't quite so satisfied. With seven mouths to feed, he needed larger prey. With an abundance of prey to choose from, his pack found and brought down a young cow elk to feast upon.

"Wait 'til y'all see what's ahead," assured Wally. "This ain't hardly nothin'."

"There's sights greater than these?" I inquired earnestly.

Wally nodded. "Yep." Enough said.

I went about stoking the fire.

"Yer Injun friend is back thar," assured Wally. "Seen him an' four ugly savages with him. No question, they be Northern Cheyenne."

Morning Star and I tried not to be alarmed at Wally's

news. I kept stoking the fire. "Appreciate the news, Wally." I pondered the weighty news. Morning Star worked at frying the fish.

"He be close enough to worry 'bout," advised Wally. "Might be prayin' this night," he added with considerable seriousness.

Morning Star and I were enjoying Wally's company. While we treasured our time alone together, the added security of the old mountain man was welcome, and his knowledge added to our appreciation for our surroundings. The fact that he'd checked our backtrail and spotted Bull Elk added immensely to his value.

We maintained our guard, lest Bull Elk catch up to us. As we sat around our small campfire, Wally regaled us with things he'd heard about this place in his travels trapping across the northern frontier. The annual rendezvous brought out an abundance of storytellers. Wally assured us that elderly Indians had been tossed into the boiling waters and emerged as young warriors. Others had quickly learned not to drink from the acidic waters. He'd been assured that the springs held medicinal qualities and been known to heal folks suffering from deadly illnesses. Wally's tales lingered on until Morning Star and I fell asleep.

We awakened to a bright sunny day with two cups of coffee sitting on red-hot coals from our cooking fire, along with a platter of the remaining fried fish. Wally was nowhere to be seen. The tracks of his mules led off to the northwest. Had he indeed left us? Or had he sensed a threat?

We devoured the remaining fish, savored the coffee, and broke camp. With Wally having gone off, Morning Star seized the opportunity to bathe in the river while I kept a lookout—mostly. We soon traded places, partly so that I wouldn't be smelling so bad. The river waters were cold and refreshing. We let the morning sun dry us before dressing and continuing our journey westward.

* * *

Unbeknownst to us, our worst nightmare had been watching us from across the river. Lust had surely been added to his driving passion to torture and kill us.

* * *

Wally was sort of right about us having seen nothing yet. We hadn't traveled all that far when we came upon another seething cauldron. This one was muddy, emitting the same rotten egg smell of the place we'd seen the day before. The combination of mud, water, and gas was impressive.

Chapter 6

Comeuppance

"Do you feel it?" I asked Morning Star as she rode beside me.

She nodded. There was no fear in her eyes. "It is time," she stated emphatically.

Vast tablelands of tall grasses lay ahead of us. We were at the southern hills of what was called the Washburn Range. Shelter was lacking for us, but such was the case for Bull Elk. I reckoned he'd gotten reinforcements and outnumbered us at least two to one, maybe more, but he wasn't so full of hatred as to be foolhardy.

We picked up our pace. Now and then, we'd look back but saw no sign of Bull Elk. Also, there was no sign of Wally. With his having headed northward likely to some imagined rendezvous, we hadn't seen hide nor hair of him.

"Look for a place to defend," I advised, with a knowing look to Morning Star. There were stands of cottonwood and aspen at these lower elevations. The fact that Bull Elk wasn't in sight didn't necessarily mean that he wasn't close. I felt it in my bones.

Paint and the mare desperately needed rest and water. We came upon a small creek and took advantage of it while scanning our backtrail. My own anxiety was taking a considerable edge from our enjoyment of the landscape.

"We be careful. Hotamo'e no win." I was so glad that Morning Star had taken to the English language so quickly. I was even more glad that she was confident in our capability to defend ourselves.

We likely had more firepower than Bull Elk, so what we lacked in numbers was partly offset by our superior weapons. Of course, that assumed the savage hadn't acquired better weapons himself.

Long about mid-afternoon, we came upon a stand of cottonwood a few feet above a creek lined with willows and tall grasses. The place even featured a beaver lodge that served to partially restrain the waters of the creek. It offered an unobstructed view of our backtrail, so we decided to cold camp at the place. I craved coffee, but there was no point in making our location obvious.

By now, I reckoned that Bull Elk must have known that we were aware of his presence. Now, it was a game of hunter and hunted. As my pa always advised, being the hunter was preferable to being the prey. As we'd journeyed across what mostly amounted to tablelands, I'd been thinking on a way to turn the tables on Bull Elk.

"I have a way to beat Hotamo'e," I declared as Morning Star was unsaddling her mare.

"How, Isa?" she said curiously.

"We will set our camp and build a bigger fire."

She gave me an incredulous look. Then, she realized what I was up to. It was an old trick. Would Bull Elk fall for it?

As night fell, we were confident that our campfire

could be seen for many miles across the tablelands. Would Bull Elk be drawn to its flames? Would the hatred possessed by the rogue Northern Cheyenne warrior overcome any caution? He'd traveled a long way in his desire to kill us, his prey.

We puffed up our bedroll. We only used the one, and it had to be convincing. We also had to be sure that Taabe and his pack stayed away. Blessedly, our wolf companions must have sensed our strategy, as the pack joined us higher up among the trees. We had a clear line of sight to the campsite. We'd have our carbines ready, though we didn't rule out the silent killer: our bows and arrows. If we could quickly and quietly eliminate a couple of Bull Elk's band with well-placed arrows, it would even the odds. Importantly, we would become the hunters. This drama would not end until Bull Elk was eliminated.

We sat among the trees, taking turns napping, while Bull Elk decided what he would do. I prayed earnestly that his crazed hatred for us would overwhelm any good sense. I was sure that he was experiencing a rush of excitement at the possibility that lay before him. If he was of a mind to torture and kill us, he'd have to enter the camp and capture us. Would he sense the trap?

The night sky was swathed in the light of what seemed to be millions of stars. A full moon added to the glow across the landscape. Wildlife was restless, as coyotes howled in the distance and an occasional owl hoot reached our ears.

I figure it was after midnight when I found cause to nudge Morning Star. As she opened her eyes, I nodded my head toward the campsite.

Five shadowy figures loomed at the edge of the circle of light. Bull Elk acted suspicious, as though unsure of a trap. This was too easy, so he'd become especially wary. He was dressed in full war regalia with his face painted white in concert with some spiritual rite.

I'd snuck down an hour earlier and heaped more wood on the fire, so the flames cast a respectable amount of light.

Bull Elk remained wary, but looked to be gaining confidence. He sent one of his warriors forward to investigate our bedroll.

I nodded to Morning Star. I'd take the warrior approaching the bedroll while she would shoot at the cluster around Bull Elk. We nocked our arrows. We each had a second shaft at the ready, but after the first arrows, we reckoned to turn to the carbines. We let fly simultaneously. There was a quick twang and the whoosh of arrows. My target caught an arrow deep in his chest as he stood over our bedroll. A savage beside Bull Elk took Morning Star's arrow deep into his neck. Both warriors lay on the ground, writhing in the pain of slow death.

Bull Elk strained to see where the arrows had come from. His eyes were unable to adjust from the brightness of our campfire to the darkness of our hiding place. He gave a brief consideration to moving blindly toward us.

We had just picked up our carbines when the boom of a flintlock tore the night apart. A third member of Bull Elk's band fell. The savage had taken the lead ball through the center of his chest and lay on the ground bleeding to death. Mercifully, he wouldn't last long. Now outnumbered and realizing he was now the prey, Bull Elk yelled a crazed war whoop and ran away from us as fast as his legs could carry him.

Morning Star and I began levering rounds into our carbines. We heard the scream of either Bull Elk or his remaining warrior take a bullet. The air quickly filled with the acrid smell of gunsmoke. We cautiously emerged from hiding with our carbines ready to fire.

"Did we kill Hotamo'e?" asked Morning Star.

"Not sure," I replied. "I think Wally is back." I figured that accounted for the booming sound of the trusty old flintlock.

Sure enough, Wally walked easy-like down from his hiding place just above us. If Bull Elk had been smarter, he'd have sent a couple of his band up to where Wally had situated himself. The rogue Cheyenne might have seen a different outcome.

"Happy to see you, friend," I expressed to the mountain man. "Nice shooting."

Wally shook his head. "Too dark to know if yer savage got away," he solemnly observed.

The question of the moment had certainly been raised. Did we kill Bull Elk? Dared we pursue our prey in the dark? Was he dead or wounded? We rightly feared that if Bull Elk was out there, he could still do some damage. "Let's put the fire out and keep a watch until morning," I said.

"Good thinkin'," agreed Wally.

Taabe and his pack emerged and began sniffing around the three dead Cheyenne. By the time the pack was done with them, there'd be no recovering bodies for burial. Blessedly, the pack dragged the carcasses off into the darkness. This was part of the wildness of the frontier. When Taabe and the pack were done, the coyotes and eventually the buzzards would finish.

The actions of Taabe's pack left us wondering what became of Bull Elk. Was he lying out there in the dark, wounded, or had he been killed? Worse, had he escaped? Or was one of his band lying out in the moonlit night?

* * *

As the sun greeted us with shards of light, I nudged Morning Star and motioned that we check the outcome of last night's battle. I gave Wally a gentle push with my foot.

We made certain our carbines were loaded and headed out along the path we figured the two Cheyenne had run. About a hundred feet from our campsite, I spotted blood. It was drying, but was of a deep red and of a quantity that indicated the likelihood of a mortal wound.

"Likely din't git far," observed Wally in a low, gravelly tone. He was a sight to behold in the mornings with his scraggly hair and near-toothless smile. But the old mountain man was as wary as ever.

"We have some tracking ahead," I whispered.

Morning Star pointed to the blood trail heading toward a stand of aspens. Four horses pranced around about a hundred yards from us. Someone had gotten away. Who remained?

I chambered a round and took the lead. At about half the distance to the horses, I saw the top of a head leaning against a tree. Drawing closer, I could make out white warpaint covering the face and body. It was Bull Elk. His mouth hung open, and there was no breathing. He was very dead. Even in death, he'd been prepared to deal his havoc. He'd propped himself against a tree with a Colt revolver gripped in his hand. Now, it lay uselessly across his lap. Bull Elk's remaining warrior must have ridden away. He'd live to tell other Northern Cheyenne and perhaps Dull Knife himself of Bull Elk's demise.

We breathed a collective sigh of relief. One of our bullets had brought Bull Elk to his end. The hunted had become the hunters and delivered the rogue savage's comeuppance.

"He no deserve burial," ventured Morning Star. "He evil. He of devil."

Wally and I nodded agreement. "Let's free the ponies and leave this place," I said.

Chapter 7

Decisions

Wally felt as though he'd done his duty to protect us as best he could. His warning about Bull Elk's nearness had certainly helped accomplish that. Wally was basically a lone wolf, and being a travel guide wasn't in his nature. He told us what lay ahead. He informed us that what the Shoshone called spouts were called geysers. One of them was apparently quite spectacular and shot up on a regular schedule. Wally finally took his leave, though I felt as though we hadn't seen the last of him. He'd spend his remaining years doing what he loved.

Wally's departure left me with decisions. There was still my vision quest, which continued ever onward so far as I could figure. Unless I had missed a clue, my life mission hadn't fallen into my quiver. And there was Morning Star. What did she seek from life? In all the banter of love, we'd focused on my vision quest. I decided it was high time to discuss her vision for our future.

That night, as we lay beneath a star-studded moonless sky, I lovingly looked down at Morning Star nestled beside me. "After we have seen the great spout the Shoshone told us of, what then? What is Awentia's desire?"

"Desire?" she replied softly.

"Yes. We always talk about my vision quest, but is that what you seek?"

It was as though she had never considered her own wants and desires. She was so caught up in her love for me, that she selflessly tied herself to my dreams. Her eyes came to new life as she pondered my question.

She gazed at me with a depth that I felt to my inner core. This was my warrior wife, the woman who'd slain enemy warriors, who'd escaped with me from the dire threat of our burning cabin, who hunted and fended off dangerous predatory beasts, and stood up to the likes of Crazy Horse and her father.

"Home and children," she finally responded.

I wasn't sure I'd rightly heard what she said. My warrior wife sought domestication? My eyes turned to the stars. A shooting star blazed across the sky. My pa said they were called meteors by folks who knew about those things. Well, the meteor was like the punctuation mark at the end of a sentence. As I gazed out upon God's vast, bejeweled creation, the answer to my vision quest came to me like a bolt from the heavens—in this case, maybe it was a meteor. "A ranch?" I ventured.

"Like George," she responded, a dreamy expression sweeping across her face.

"We could go to Texas," I suggested. "Not so much snow."

"Does Isa like Texas?" she asked.

I gazed up at the spectacular panoply extending from horizon to horizon. But for the added majesty of the mountains, the night sky was every bit as big as back in

Texas. There was cold to be dealt with down south, but nothing so brutal as the bitter cold and deep snows here. Was it simply a question of the weather? George and Running Waters had certainly learned to deal with it. The tribes were no more friendly or hostile in Texas, and prejudices ran thick pretty much everywhere. Wherever we decided to settle, I felt drawn to wide open spaces. The fewer folks that had to be dealt with, the better. "We don't have to live in Texas."

"Awentia go where Isa go," she said as she pulled close to me.

This was surely the love between man and woman that God talked about. As I pondered an answer to where we might settle down, an idea struck me like a bolt from the sky. Maybe that meteor was doing double duty. More likely, my vision quest was coming to an end. "Two ranches," I mused.

Morning Star held up two fingers with a questioning expression.

I nodded. "Two. One in Wyoming and one in Texas. We can drive cattle north in the spring, spend the summer here, and return to Texas in the fall. I aim to raise and train Quarter Horses, too."

"Why not all of horse?" asked Morning Star.

I wasn't sure whether she was joking, then realized she thought I was talking about part of a horse. "It's the name of a breed, a type of horse. Cowboys love them. They are strong, fast, and smart. Raising and training them would be a good business," I explained.

"Business?"

"We sell cattle and horses for money. The price must be greater than the cost to raise them, so there's money to buy supplies and raise and feed more livestock." She was still giving me that questioning look. I'd opened a new world to her. Hers had been one of trading goods for goods. The idea of money as representing value was a foreign concept. Here we were living off the land on a journey to some unknown destination. If we wanted something, we killed it, found it among the flora, or traded for it. "We can still hunt and trade."

Morning Star nodded tentatively. "Money," she stated with an uncertain tone.

"It's part of the White world, like owning land. Like most things we can own, God advises us not to worship it." I searched my feeble brain for an example. "Gold is like money. Men come to find it. They collect as much as they can. When they are driven to take gold from others, it is called greed. It is an evil that kills bodies and spirits."

"If evil, why have money?" she persisted.

This was a great question. "Because money is a means of trade. It represents the value of what is being sold. Like one longhorn might be valued at one hundred dollars, but a thousand longhorns would be valued at one hundred thousand dollars or more."

Morning Star nodded. She was beginning to understand.

"What we do when we have money?"

Now, there was a great question. "When we have enough to live and raise a family, we will use it to help others who don't have so much." My pa had driven this lesson home from the time we'd grown to his waistline.

Morning Star nestled more tightly under my arm. "We go to big spout. Make ranch later." She looked into my eyes. "Awentia love Isa."

Now, it was just the two of us. Bull Elk was no longer a threat, and Wally had headed off to his mythical rendezvous. The decision we had reached added greater peace to our journey. If all went well, we'd see the great spout and return to George's ranch before the weather turned cold. There'd be time to rebuild our cabin and look for land upon which we could build a ranch and a future.

My mind was already working on the new cabin. After watching it go up in flames and recalling my pa's story of seeing his family's log and plank cabin burned to the ground, I was determined to build our new home with rock. I recalled the biblical tale of building a house on sand versus rock, so this sort of paralleled that story. Of course, Christ was talking about a church. In my mind, my faith and that of Morning Star were sort of like a church, especially as we built our family. In fact, it came to mind that Fort Laramie might not be around forever, and it was time to think about establishing some sort of town. We could start with a trading post. I chuckled to myself, as I imagined adding a boarding house, smithy shop, church, jail, and schoolhouse. A train depot might be a possibility.

"What Isa think?" Morning Star had been watching me intently and sensed that I was dreaming of the future. It still amazed me that her thoughts mingled so easily with mine.

"I'm reckoning to build our house of rock."

She nodded. "Rock not burn. Good."

I turned to saddle Paint, and Morning Star grabbed my arm.

She looked up at me dreamily. "We make big house. Big family, many friends." The love of my life had already given our future home plenty of thought. "Yes?"

I leaned in and kissed her. "Yes." I helped her pack our gear on the horses, and we were soon mounted up and headed west toward what the Shoshone had described as a big spout.

* * *

Oh, that our travels would be so easy. The central plateau over which we now traversed tended to lull travelers with its mile after mile of sameness. There's a boredom about it that tends to have a relaxing effect, which in turn can make a traveler less attentive toward potential threats. We hadn't ridden more than a couple of miles and were about to cross a small stream when movement off to our left caught our attention. Large male grizzlies, what folks called boars, were rather hard to miss. We had come upon one. He'd been fishing and looked to be a tad annoyed at us interrupting his pleasure. He became even more irritated at the sight of the pack of wolves following us. While I doubted Taabe was interested, the grizzly would take no chances. He stood to afford himself a better look at us. Big? He was huge.

I figured the grizzly to be overreacting until I spotted his mate and two cubs about a hundred yards ahead of us. Morning Star and I looked knowingly at each other. The instinct to protect one's young was deeply embedded in all living things. I motioned for us to head off to our right, staying well clear of the grizzlies.

We hadn't gone but a couple of hundred yards, when we encountered another grizzly family. It seemed that we'd arrived at the wrong place at the wrong time. It was like a rendezvous of grizzlies! Continuing in the direction we'd chosen was now out of the question unless we planned to take on the grizzlies. I looked back at Taabe and could see that he had set his pack in a defensive formation. His great furry head was up and alert with those great blue eyes casting a penetrating glare toward the boar grizzly ahead of us. Taabe was ready for a fight, if the situation came to a battle. It wasn't lost on me that he had three young pups to protect.

The second male grizzly stood to get a better look at us. He had to be at least nine feet tall. I didn't even want to imagine what a swipe of those three-inch claws would do to human flesh.

We seemed to be at a standoff. Morning Star and I looked to our rear, but our escape was now cut off by the first bear having moved near the route we'd have to take. "This not good," observed Morning Star. Her understatement was more a consequence of nerves than an attempt at humor.

There were no stands of trees to retreat to. We were out in the middle of a grassy plateau intersected by the stream. In short, we were exposed. I drew my Spencer from its scabbard. I didn't want to needlessly kill any bears, but I did not intend for us to be on their dining menu. Morning Star held her Henry across her saddle horn. We'd both chambered rounds and began backing our horses to within Taabe's defensive perimeter.

Time seemed to slow to a crawl. I nervously fingered my mountain lion claw necklace with its carved wooden cross. I wasn't anxious to be making a bear claw necklace, assuming we would win any scrap with these beasts. "Lord protect us," I kept whispering to myself.

What happened next came as a total surprise. The first male grizzly charged the second. A territorial dispute had begun. I had forgotten Buffalo Man's advice on how grizzlies were highly protective of their territory. The first grizzly was the larger of the two and plowed with his full weight into the second boar. The fight was on!

I quickly scanned the area in search of an escape route. The sow and two cubs of the first grizzly had moved further away to avoid the battle. The sows snarled and made threatening paw swipes but seemed more interested in protecting their cubs. "Let's go!" I said to Morning Star and led us past the spot where the first grizzly had been fishing. We whipped Paint and the mare to full speed with Taabe's pack following close behind. We were intent on putting considerable distance between us and the great battle raging behind us at the stream.

We found a stand of cottonwoods about a mile beyond our encounters with the bears and pulled up to give our mounts a breather.

"Isa strong *sunipu,*" observed Morning Star.

I laughed. "Praise God that the bears fought each other and not us," I stated.

Morning Star gave me a quizzical look.

"If the grizzlies had attacked us, they would have died. They will fight each other but not kill."

She smiled. "Isa wise."

I had to admit to knowing more about the ways of wildlife than I realized. I'd had good teachers.

We decided to walk the horses a piece. Sometimes being on foot was a welcome contrast to sitting astride a gently rocking saddle.

Chapter 8

Big Spout

We had ridden to a great stand of pine and stopped just shy of a steep drop. Below us was a great waterfall. The waters rushed down in an awesome display of power. The steepness of the canton walls and depth of the drop from our perch high above was awe-inspiring.

"Shoshone say this Firehole River," said Morning Star. "Great spout that way," she added, pointing to our south. Our chosen path had apparently taken us too far to the north.

I was impressed that my warrior wife had so fully absorbed the descriptions provided by the Shoshone. The overlook upon which we stood gave us a birds-eye view of the falls and the rushing rapids below. We dismounted, sat on a fallen log, and breathed deeply of the crisp mountain air. We sat silently for a few moments, enjoying the falls and our own companionship.

There was a singular beauty about this place that inspired both of us. Lush grasses and tall lodgepole pine trees grew in abundance, with juniper, a smattering of aspen, and birch. Game was plentiful. I looked high on a nearly ridge line and spotted an immense bull elk in a majestic pose as though king of all he surveyed. Grizzlies seemed ever-present, and we took a wide berth of them. With a sigh, we mounted up and headed Paint and the mare southward. As we followed the river, there were plenty of buffalo. Rising columns of steam were reminders of the ever-present hot springs. For those unintimidated by the hot springs and pools, challenging game trails, and occasional geysers, a great life could be carved from this wondrous place. God had surely blessed it. The terrain had now become decidedly rougher than the great plateau we'd traversed. While we were intent on taking in all of the spectacle of the region, we nevertheless now had a reason for returning to George's ranch sooner than later.

We followed the river over the next couple of days, journeying southward along its east bank. The trek was arduous, to say the least. We came upon several of the erupting geysers that the Shoshones called spouts. I decided that geyser sounded more descriptive.

We finally arrived at a place where the river took a turn eastward.

"Shoshone say big spout close to this place," observed Morning Star.

I was ready. We'd come a long way in anticipation of the sight of this great geyser spouting, which the Shoshone were so excited by. The sun was at its zenith, as we continued to follow the crystalline waters of the Firehole River.

We rode and walked for a few more hours. The sun was closing in on the western horizon, so we began to think about stopping for the night. We had gone a bit further, when the horses began acting nervous. "Let's walk," I said. As my feet hit the ground, I felt a very faint vibration. No wonder the horses had become skittish.

As Morning Star alighted from the mare, she gave me a knowing look. "We close," she said.

Geysers and hot springs had continually been revealed to our ever-wondering eyes, but none matched the aroma of sulfur and sounds of the earth building pressure beneath us. Vibrant blues and bright oranges decorated many of its mud pots and hot springs. We were tired but determined to see this wondrous sight that Wally and the Shoshones told us about. Besides, there were no bears or other beasts to interrupt our idyll. "This must be the place," I said. We rounded a bend and came upon what appeared to be a large open rise covered in a whitish residue. We'd become used to such treeless scenes, but none quite like this.

We settled onto a log along a nearby tree line. The Shoshone had said this great spout was distinguished from others by the regularity of its eruptions. Wally said they occurred what seemed like every hour or so. Taabe and his pack had followed and joined us. They seemed just as anxious with anticipation as us.

"We camp here?" asked Morning Star.

I shrugged. The area seemed safe enough. I hesitated a tad, as the vibrations seemed to be weakening. "Yes. We camp here," I repeated.

We began to unpack the horses, though I was concerned that they were still a tad jittery. I didn't want them running off, so I decided to tether them to a couple of nearby trees with enough line to feed comfortably.

Morning Star busied herself with setting up our

campsite while I hunted for some wood for a cooking fire. We reckoned to roast the last of some venison from a deer I'd killed two days back. I'd not even gotten a fire started, when a roar filled the air. We turned awestruck to see a geyser spouting high into the air. The watery column was easily more than a hundred feet high. Morning Star and I embraced as much as a reflexive reaction as a deep desire to enjoy the stunning sight together. The Shoshone had definitely not disappointed us.

The eruption lasted just a couple of minutes.

The horses endured the event, so we felt relaxed.

"Let's move our campsite further away," I suggested, pointing toward a thick stand of lodgepole pine a couple of hundred yards away.

Morning Star looked from me to where the geyser had erupted and nodded vigorously.

We gathered our cam equipment and hauled it to the trees, where I found a small clearing and rebuilt our cooking fire. As we cooked the venison, another eruption sent showers of boiling water skyward. "We stay here," I said, as much a statement as a question.

"We stay," replied Morning Star. We were soon enjoying our venison. As a celebration, we brewed the last of the coffee Wally had given us. The first star began to show in the darkening sky, so we began to lay out our bedroll. The vibration began again. We exchanged a questioning glance that asked whether this was a regular occurrence? We extinguished the cooking fire and were just about to turn in, when the geyser erupted again.

The regularity of the event was surely confirmed, and we would be treated to eruptions all night long. They weren't alarming enough to be concerning, but this regularity was new to us and kept us unsettled. The surrounding territory was too unfamiliar to travel at night, so we endured the geyser's eruptions through the night. The experience was memorable to say the least. Enjoying the beauty of the geyser spouting high had turned into a bit of an annoyance at night.

"We leave before sun," said Morning Star.

I agreed. The first glow of light dancing across the eastern sky would offer enough for us to see our way eastward.

* * *

Just as we left the big geyser, it offered up a parting blast that served to pick up our pace a bit. It had been a restless night of frequently interrupted sleep. It had been an experience ever seared into our memories. From what I sensed of their nervous excitement, Paint and Morning Star's mare shared our aim of putting the geyser behind us sooner than later.

We headed due east, calculating that it would eventually take us to the place where the lake fed the Yellowstone River. Facing the rising sun on a chilly summer morning, high in the mountains, had a certain romance to it. Morning Star and I were now driven by our aim to get back to George's ranch and begin the future that had been revealed to us. Establishing and maintaining two ranches was a huge undertaking, but we were confident...perhaps, overly so.

The terrain remained rugged, and it took us about a full day to reach the far western reaches of Yellowstone Lake. It was my understanding that this is where we crossed the Continental Divide demarked the watersheds between east and west. To the west, waters shed toward the Pacific Ocean, while waters to the east headed toward the Atlantic Ocean. Importantly, we would now follow the north shore of the lake to the Yellowstone River.

We saw plenty of wildlife. Bears were in abundance along with elk, deer, bighorn sheep, buffalo, eagles, and plenty more. It was like God's great cornucopia of life. It was hard not to constantly scan the landscape as we traveled. That posed its own challenge, as we had to remain ever alert for human predators.

By now, we had developed a good feel for avoiding confrontations with the beasts of the wild. Our previous encounter with the bears fighting over territory was a prime example for our education.

There is little to match the experiences of viewing God's creatures in their element. Watching an eagle swoop to deftly pluck a fish from the lake or a mountain lion to bring down an elk calf served to add to our ever-fuller appreciation for the chain of life.

So it was that we found ourselves mesmerized by a pair of bighorn rams battling. They'd come together with a loud crack of horns meeting horns, then they'd back away to shake off the collision before charging at each other again. It was about dominance and mating rights.

"Head hurts," laughed Morning Star.

I joined in her laughter. "One of them will win," I observed. My words hung in my mind. There were winners and losers everywhere. What did it take to win? With the bighorn sheep, the stronger ram would go on to reproduce his kind. The loser would slink off to possibly try again.

It occurred to me that we hadn't seen a soul since Wally departed. We occasionally split off and examined our backtrail, but it didn't appear that anyone was following us. We scanned our surroundings but saw only the wildlife. Still, there was my sense that a threat lurked. I reckoned that was a good thing, as it raised the level of my vigilance. Occasionally, I'd turn to Morning Star, and I noted that she also sensed something. It was unspoken between us, yet we shared the gift of heightened consciousness.

We were both in our saddles, when I reined Paint to a halt. I put a finger to my lips and shifted my eyes off to our left, away from the lake.

I reached for my Spencer carbine, as Morning Star nodded imperceptibly and duplicated my action by pulling her Henry carbine from its scabbard.

We peered intently into the dense stand of pine slightly above our position. If anyone was hiding, it surely provided them with great cover.

"Wagh! Dagnabbit!" came a familiar voice.

"Wally?" I called.

"Been followin' y'all fer nigh unto an hour without yuh knowin'," he exclaimed with a broad grin. "Not bad fer this old fella." He emerged from the trees with mules in tow.

"We thought you were looking for the rendezvous," offered Morning Star.

"Aw, shucks. I ain't thet fur gone. I knows there be no vous." He laughed heartily. "I reckoned I'd have a bit of fun with y'all an' see how long it'd take fer yuh to spot me." He laughed some more. As he stepped toward us, an arrow from deeper in the trees plowed through his shoulder. "Dang!" he hollered. "Fergot 'bout them Crows!"

We dove from our horses, slapped their rumps, and ran for what little cover the shoreline of the lake gave us.

Wally staggered and then mostly tumbled the fifty feet or so distance and settled in beside us. From what I could figure, Wally thought he'd evaded some angry Crow that were in pursuit. While I was thinking on it, a couple of arrows sailed over our heads and skimmed off the lake water surface.

"What do they want?" I asked Wally. The Crow were normally peaceful, as I learned while serving as a scout on the Yellowstone Expedition.

"The hotheads think I stole their dinner," he responded.

"Did you?"

"Well, it was only half cooked an' I was hungry," he confessed.

"How many are there?" I hissed with a touch of anger at the predicament Wally had placed us in.

"Three, mebbe four," responded Wally.

"*Cheyakh,*" called out Morning Star. She turned to me. "Is Crow word for peace."

Hearing their native tongue, the Crow paused their attack.

I laid my carbine aside and stood. "*Kola,*" I said in Lakota.

The Crow had now heard their own language spoken, and now the Lakota word for friend. One of them stepped from the trees. "*WíiyawA wíiyA hwo,*" he explained in Lakota that they wanted the White man.

I pointed to Wally. "*Kola,*" I said.

The Crow warrior nocked an arrow in his bowstring.

As the warrior drew back his bowstring, I caught sight of a doe off to my left. I swiftly picked up my Spencer, aimed, and felled the deer.

The totally surprised Crow nearly lost his grip on the bow.

That had been quite an attention getter. I pointed to myself. "Isa O'toole...*kola* Crow." I gestured toward Morning Star. "Awentia Miniconjou Lakota. *Kola*." I hoped I was getting our message across.

Wally just sat there taking it all in with the arrow stuck through his shoulder. "I only took a couple of bites," he lamented. "I left most of it."

The Crow put the arrow back in his quiver. He and his companions weren't about to take on our carbines. They looked hungrily at the dead doe.

Morning Star arose and stood beside me as I made a sign to eat and motioned the Crow to come join us. Inside, I was thanking God for delivering that hapless doe at precisely the right moment.

The Crow didn't look especially kindly at Wally, but he seemed to be out of danger from them. While I built a fire, Morning Star began tending to Wally's shoulder.

The Crow quickly field-dressed the deer and began carving it for roasting. They were well into their efforts, when Taabe and his pack appeared. The Crow stood back aghast with surprise before going for their bows.

"No!" I commanded. The pack trotted over to me, and I ruffled Taabe's mane.

The Crow facial expressions changed dramatically from fear to amazement at what they perceived as my power over the wolf pack. They babbled among themselves in the Crow tongue and looked at me with obvious respect.

Morning Star paused from tending to Wally's wound and doubled the perception of strong medicine by hugging Taabe's mate, Mua.

The Crow warriors were impressed. They were apparently awed sufficiently to forgive Wally, as one of the warriors stepped forward to help Morning Star with the old mountain man's wound while the other two finished carving up the deer. The Crow went about removing the arrow while Morning Star put together a healing poultice.

Wally? The old codger took it in with a smile despite any pain. I expect he appreciated the attention coupled with the relief in realizing that the Crow were no longer looking to lift his hair.

Soon enough, we were all gathered around the campfire in animated conversation and enjoying venison steaks while imbibing of Wally's coffee. The Crow thought it a strange brew, but seemed to enjoy it.

The Crow reinforced rumors I had heard that Red Cloud and Sitting Bull, along with Crazy Horse, were talking about assembling the tribes to take on the invading Whites. Apparently, Yellow Hair's expedition into the Black Hills was stirring up the tribes. I had heard from Tathanka that Custer had been given the nickname about eight years back during what was called Red Cloud's War, when the cavalryman served under Major General Winfield Scott Hancock. Custer's deceptive interactions with the Southern Cheyenne Chief, Black Kettle, was followed by his responsibility for the slaughter of dozens of Cheyenne and Arapaho at what was called the Washita Massacre. Notably, Black Kettle had survived a previous massacre at Sand Creek but had been lured into accepting the White man's promises of peace. The broken promises of the White man were bringing the tribes to a fever pitch.

The Crow told stories of attacking homesteads and wagon trains, but fears of retribution by the blue coats hung heavily over the aggression. Lieutenant Colonel George Custer seemed to do what he could to feed those fears. Nevertheless, the tales told by these warriors served to put Morning Star and me on alert as we formed our plans for building a ranch near Fort Laramie. We'd also be extra vigilant on our journey. In fact, I wondered what our interaction with the normally peaceful Crow might have been like if there were a couple of dozen warriors chasing Wally. Our extra firepower likely would not have been enough.

The coffee pot was soon empty, and what little remained of the doe went to Taabe and his pack. The now-graciously respectful Crow departed with much friendly sign. Wally even gave them a pouch filled with coffee beans, having shown them how to brew the bitter drink.

"That were right close," observed Wally after the Crow were out of sight. "I let my hungries git the best of me an' got careless."

Morning Star and I shook our heads. There was no remorse in the mountain man. If he wasn't so generally likable, we'd have been very upset with him.

Wally stood, winced at a stab of pain from his wound, and stared at us a moment. We had fashioned a makeshift sling to relieve pressure on his shoulder. "Thanks fer yer help. I'd best be movin' on." There was no arguing with Wally. He was an independent cuss who didn't care to be dependent on anyone. He'd manage despite his wound.

"Careful you don't open that wound, Wally." I'd already told him to take it easy for a few days, but I might as well have been talking to a rock wall for all my advice mattered.

Wally paused and stared at Morning Star and me. He looked to have a heavy heart. "Back when I was a young whippersnapper, I knew this day would come. Folks keep comin' west. Most be well meanin'. We be gettin' buried in the dust of wagon wheels an' folks startin' new lives. Bufler keep gettin' pushed west. Folks find a place to put down roots, mebbe a stream, a stand of purty trees, a meadow. Comes a house an' plantin', mebbe a tradin' post, add a church, a schoolhouse, the law, an' soon nuf they got them a town. Then they build another an' another. It be enough tuh clog yer head and stop yer breathin'."

I nodded. It was happening before our eyes. How could I not agree?

"Sure as thet old sun rise an' set, them Injuns seen what be hapnin'. Figured fer a bit thet I might escape by trappin' higher an' higher in them mountains. But we all be gettin' crowded out. Hoped it might not happin', but I be dead wrong. You and yer woman here have the answers. Use the land fer good ends, respect folks of all colors, love, build yerselfs a family."

Morning Star gave Wally a gentle hug and handed him some poultice wrapped in the skin of the doe we'd killed. I shared a long handshake with the old mountain man.

Wally gathered his mules and was soon headed off to do whatever pleased his aging bones and still fertile mind.

I looked up at the sun hanging well above the western horizon. We still had time to cover a few miles before making camp. I looked at Morning Star as she finished saddling the mare. I was a lucky man to have found this woman, this warrior wife who stood by my side in facing down the Crow. It led me to better understand the bond between my parents.

"What think?" cooed Morning Star, as she watched me in my musings.

"Think?" I laughed. "Isa know."

"Know what?" she asked as though she'd already guessed my answer.

"I love you."

We mounted up and turned our horses eastward. We had a long way yet to travel.

Chapter 9

Beyond the Absaroka

It took another handful of days to reach the Absaroka Range and the pass that opened to the vast vistas beyond the bounds of Yellowstone National Park. We began a southeasterly route that would eventually intersect with the headwaters of the North Platte River and meet the Oregon Trail. We were moving into Northern Cheyenne and Sihásapas Lakota country with the attendant need for vigilance.

With game plentiful, we never experienced hunger. We didn't take on a buffalo again, but enjoyed elk, deer, rabbit, and even an overly inquisitive coyote. The streams we crossed enabled us to add fish to our diet. We'd also become expert in the natural edible vegetation along our route. God's provisions were abundant.

Over the next ten days, we saw no other humans. Paint and the mare were sure-footed as we negotiated often exceedingly rugged terrain. Some folks likely would have been put off by the silent serenity of our journey. Other than crossing the rushing waters of a couple of rivers, our travels were peaceful. Days were colored by crystal-clear skies and breezes that carried fragrant aromas of flowers and ever-plentiful lodgepole pines and junipers. The sounds of wildlife echoed symphonically in our ears. Until a person has had the opportunity to simply enjoy the sights and sounds of this vast frontier, they cannot begin to appreciate its sheer wonder. The majesty of snow-capped peaks under azure skies, lush forests contrasted with rolling flowered plains, and rushing streams serve as a constant reminder of the freedom we enjoyed. We made the love talk that such surroundings inspired and spoke of the beautiful home we'd build here in Wyoming. God had gifted me with a vision quest that would lift Morning Star and me to our future together.

The headwaters of the North Platte came into view. We were nearing the end of August. Our dallying amid the beauty of Yellowstone National Park had consumed precious time, but it had been worth every second.

We spotted two hunting parties over the next couple of days. Both bands were Hunkpapa Lakota, so there was naught but friendly acknowledgment. The Lakota complained that the large herds of buffalo were becoming more difficult to find.

* * *

I suppose it could be said that we were leading a charmed life. Two well-armed travelers accompanied by a wolf pack were not attractive prey. We were nearing the Oregon Trail, when we ran into a touch of trouble.

We were cold camped about five days from what travelers called the Emigrant's Wash Tub, a place on the Oregon Trail where settlers paused their wagon trains to water livestock, do laundry, and bathe. We'd laid out our bedroll under a full moon, and Morning Star took first watch. She sat next to me, cradling her Henry carbine, while I caught some shuteye. Taabe and his pack were roaming the surrounding territory for prey.

The crack of a broken twig brought Morning Star to alert. She gently but urgently nudged me awake.

"Who goes?" she called out and grabbed her Henry carbine.

A voice rang out from under the moonlight. "Dang, Fred, it's our lucky day! Sounds like a woman!"

"Shut yer yap, Clint. I git her first!" exclaimed Fred.

"But..."

"You were first last time!" called the man named Fred.

I grabbed my Spencer and crawled about fifteen feet from Morning Star and faced the direction from which the voices were coming. I signed to Morning Star to speak again so as to draw the men in and see what we were dealing with.

"What do you want?" called Morning Star.

The men appeared seemingly out of nowhere and stood less than twenty feet from Morning Star. "Lookee here, Clint. She's a Redskin, an' a purty squaw." The man had a rough, hangdog appearance with a threadbare wool coat and britches. A derby hat sat atop his scraggly hair. His smirk broadened to a nearly toothless smile.

"She be holdin' somethin'. What it be?" asked Clint, squinting his eyes to see better in the dimness.

They had no idea that I was near and aiming my carbine at them.

"She likely ain't got a clue how to use that there peashooter," said Fred, with an air of assurance. "Dang, but this is gonna be good. I luvs a fighter," he said, as he leered through dark eyes that seemed ever darker. He had a long nose and a weak chin that gave him the appearance of a snake. He cut about as presentable a figure as his partner, Clint. Fred gave a snort and wiped his nose with his dirt-encrusted sleeve. He reeked of the stench of sweat and liquor.

As the men came closer, Morning Star made out a deep scar across Fred's cheek that gave him an even more sinister look. She raised the Henry to where the muzzle was a mere five feet from Fred's midsection. She chambered a round.

"Yuh don't wanna be doin' any shootin', sweetie. This ain't gonna hurt a bit," ogled Fred. "I be gentle. Thet, I promise." He began to unfasten his pants.

Unlike Fred, who was focused on Morning Star, Clint heard the sound of the lever on my Spencer. "Fred! Be keerful! There be another one!"

Fred backed off and saw me off to his left. "Shoot, Clint. It's just some half-breed kid."

Clint began to bring his rifle into position but hesitated upon seeing my carbine.

Neither Morning Star nor I wanted to do any killing, but the threat we faced was forcing us to act.

An ugly sneer crossed Fred's face, as he pulled his hunting knife and took a step forward. "Yuh kin make this easy or…" Morning Star's bullet plowed through the man's stomach. The Henry's ear-splitting blast echoed across the hills.

Fred's eyes opened wide with disbelief. He lurched backward from the sheer force of the slug, looked down at his belly, and dropped helplessly to his knees. He let the knife clatter to the rocky ground.

Before Clint could react, a slug from my Spencer blew a hole just in front of his ear. He was dead before he hit the ground.

As Fred breathed his last, I rushed to Morning Star's

side and held her. It was as much for my comfort as for hers.

"Isa! Isa!" she sobbed.

We stood joined as one for a long time.

Taabe entered our camp circle and broke us up with a few licks and nuzzles. One of the pups was beginning to gnaw on Clint's leg, but Taabe turned and chased him off with a growl. I think he understood the ways of us humans.

We did as best we could to cover the bodies up with rock under some nearby aspen. The soil was simply too hard for digging graves. The worst part was dragging the corpses to the trees, as they stunk terribly. I did say a prayer over the bodies.

We were uncomfortable remaining near the scene of the attack, so we walked about a mile downstream. It was a bit of a challenge owing to the dim light, but we managed to find a satisfactory spot.

"Why, Isa?" Morning Star was once again confronted with the question of why God let bad things happen.

"God fights the evil one, sweetheart," I responded. "He gave us the power to defend ourselves. He wants us to be strong, so He tests us."

"Awentia not like tests," she lamented.

"Why God not kill evil one?"

That was a tougher question. I looked up thoughtfully at the moon. Taabe and the pack lay around us in a circle. I absentmindedly stroked Taabe's mane. "If God didn't keep us strong to defeat evil, we could not appreciate all He has given us." I was sure God didn't want us taking Him for granted. "If He didn't love us, he wouldn't have given us a way to stop the evil we faced."

She nodded and nestled closer, finally closing her eyes and falling into peaceful slumber.

* * *

Rain. Our azure skies of the past few days had clouded over and delivered rain. It wasn't of the wind-driven variety, but steady enough. We broke out oilskin coats, saddled up, and began a search for cover.

We literally stumbled onto the Oregon Trail, as Paint partly tripped on a wagon wheel rut. There were no wagon trains in sight, but plenty of evidence of their passings lingered. We soon found an abandoned wagon lying mostly tipped over. It afforded us temporary shelter from the rain.

We were impatient to continue our journey, but the rain had cooled the air considerably, and despite our oilskin jackets, our buckskins had gotten soaking wet. The wet hide had a cooling effect. I built a fire to warm and dry us as best possible. We stripped out of our wet clothes and absorbed the fire's warmth while we huddled under the wagon. Even Taabe and the pack shared our shelter. Only our ever-loyal horses endured the rain. My mind drifted to how in a couple of months from now this rain would be snow; maybe a blizzard.

The sun finally broke free of its cloudy prison, and we were able to resume our journey home. With any luck, we figured to make a dozen miles before sunset.

As we followed the trail eastward, there was a sense of the onslaught of what folks called civilization. It was the very concept that concerned the likes of Crazy Horse, Red Cloud, Sitting Bull, and other tribal leaders. I felt like an onlooker, as I lived in both White and Red worlds. The precepts of the White man's civilization were completely foreign to the tribes. I knew, as did Morning Star, that the old ways would necessarily pass. I might say that the Indians would have to accept the new ways or die, but many would die anyway as greedy opportunists connived to rob them of their heritage. We'd heard tales of Indian agents who kept much-needed food and blankets from the reservation tribes. Others shot wildlife for sport, leaving carcasses to rot in the sun.

We had dismounted to give our horses some relief, when I saw a slim pillar of smoke rising a couple of miles to the south. I pointed it out to Morning Star. "Let's see what happened," I suggested.

Morning Star nodded agreement and turned her mare to follow me.

The ground was mostly flat and grassy, so we covered the distance quickly even at a walk. A couple of cattle mooed at us as we approached the smoldering ruins of what had been a sod and log hut. The corral was empty, and there was no sign of life save for those cattle we'd passed. A dog lay dead, its throat slit. We finally came upon a man and woman staked out on the ground. They'd been horribly tortured before being relieved by death.

Morning Star freed an arrow from a dead horse and examined the shaft. "Cheyenne," she said.

I looked at the arrow and agreed.

We were both thinking the same thing and had the same answer to the why of the attack.

"Let's bury them...whoever they are," I said and grabbed a shovel that the fire had missed.

Morning Star proceeded to undertake the distasteful task of unfastening the victims from the stakes while I dug a grave for the two. They bore no identification.

"Tathanka words come true," stated Morning Star matter-of-factly, as though it was an inevitability. "People will make war on Whites," she added.

"I fear it will happen," I responded ruefully. "Many will die. It's sad."

"We are in middle," she observed. She was so right. Our planned ranch would be physically located in the heart of Indian country, but so would our life together. My being half White and half Comanche and Morning Star being a Lakota, our children would be partly White. It was a sort of symbolic mix of races. We lived in a world of mixes of this sort. George's and Running Waters' daughter Esmeralda was part Black and part Pawnee. My own brothers and sister were half White and half Comanche like me. Yet there was a world out there that held deep prejudices against what they saw as sinful racial and cultural abominations.

After burying the homesteaders, we took a final look around. There was nothing salvageable from the burned-out hulk of the cabin. What I did find set me back. It was a doll; a girl's plaything. There was no sign of a child. The Cheyenne had apparently taken the girl to either raise as their own or to torture and kill later.

I stuffed the doll in my saddlebag, figuring that someone might recognize its owner. It was a long shot, but stranger things had been known to happen on the frontier. There was also the possibility that the Cheyenne would trade the girl for food, blankets, and weapons. That would offer the best chance of her recovery from an uncertain fate.

* * *

We rode back to the Oregon Trail and continued our travels eastward. I reckoned that we were about five days from the place we would call our new home.

Long about midway through the second day since the

homestead incident, we encountered a sizable wagon train. They were in a rush to get their prairie schooners over the Continental Divide and closing in on Oregon before winter struck with its typical fury.

We must have been quite a sight for the wagon master. Our youth couldn't offset the reality that we bore the physical consequences of long days walking and riding and ever-cooler nights, grabbing sleep often on rocky beds. There we sat, a half-breed and a Lakota woman astride our horses with Taabe and his pack beside us.

The wagon train lumbered our way until the wagon master saw us. He raised his hand to halt the wagons, as his eyes bore in on our wolf companions.

"What's happening, Chuck?" We heard a voice calling to the wagon master from the lead wagon.

"Couple Injuns an' what look to be wolves!" he hollered back.

"Wolves! Injuns!" came the cry from the lead wagon. We could hear the message echo from wagon to wagon down the line.

A bunch of pioneer-type men and a couple of women quickly emerged carrying every conceivable type of rifle. You'd have thought the entire Indian nation was about to descend upon them.

Morning Star and I raised our right hands high as a sign of peace. "Hail the wagon train!" I hollered.

The fact that I spoke perfect English seemed to perplex the wagon master. "Who you be?" he called out while readying his rifle.

"I'm Isa O'Toole and this is my wife. We're headed to George Freeman's ranch near Fort Laramie."

Using George's name must have been a positive,

because the wagon master eased up with his rifle. "Freeman's ranch, you say?"

"Yes. We're friends."

"Come in real slow like," invited the wagon master with suspicion still lingering in his eyes.

"You trustin' then Injuns, Chuck?" called out one of the pioneer folks.

Morning Star and I urged our horses toward the wagon master.

Chuck sported a broad grin, as we approached. "Y'all related to a fella named Jack O'Toole?"

"He's my pa," I responded.

"Wal shucks. He still ranchin' down Texas way?" asked the wagon master.

"You okay, Chuck?" hollered out another settler.

"Hold yer britches," replied Chuck. "These folks be okay."

"Where do you know my pa from?" I asked.

"I spent a bit of time ridin' for Captain Rip Ford as a Texas Ranger. Yer pa and an Injun did some scoutin' fer Rip. Yer pa's a good man. So was the Injun." Chuck smiled, as he recollected his time with the famed Texas Ranger captain from two decades past. "Y'all headin' fer George's ranch, eh?"

We nodded in unison while keeping a wary eye on the still-suspicious wagon train folks. "We're going to build a ranch near his place."

"Well, George is a right fine man. He helped us with a couple of axle problems. Yep, right generous."

"Y'all might be extra careful ahead. Cheyenne are on the warpath. A homestead a few miles back got burned out. The man and woman were killed, and it looked like their daughter was taken." I pulled the doll from my saddlebag. "We'll be looking for the little girl that goes with this," I added sorrowfully.

"Thet be a cryin' shame," lamented the wagon master. "Appreciate the warnin'. Do y'all be needin' anythin'?"

"Thanks kindly. We're close to home." I reckoned the wagon train would be stopping at the foothills of the Laramie Range near where the soldiers from Fort Laramie cut timber to use in building the fort. There was no point in delaying their journey, and we didn't figure to backtrack.

Chuck waved the travelers back to their wagons and turned back to us. "You two look like yuh bin doin' a bit of travelin'," he observed.

"We see place called Yellowstone National Park. Much magic," said Morning Star with a smile.

Chuck's eyes widened at Morning Star's near-perfect English. "I heard of it. Injuns say there be big spouts. Guess I owe it a visit." He smiled longingly. "Meanwhile, I gotta git these folks to Oregon. Time's a-wastin'." He tipped his hat, turned westward, and signaled the wagon train to move out.

We moved off to the side of the trail as the prairie schooners began lumbering up the trail. We caught all sorts of looks from the settlers. The children were especially curious, laughing and prancing along beside their wagons as their parents warned them to keep a safe distance from the two wild-looking apparitions. I shook my head at a couple of wagons that were obviously overloaded. They'd never make it over the mountainous terrain that lay ahead. It was amazing that they'd gotten this far.

We watched about twenty wagons roll past. Oxen strained at their yokes, the air was broken by the occasional crack of a whip, mules brayed, a woman with long walking sticks ambled along beside the wagons, and horses whinnied and snorted, as the caravan went on its way. I sure felt considerable respect for these folks, as they pursued dreams of a fresh start. Opportunity sure beckoned. I suppose it was that way with Morning Star and me, except we weren't with a wagon train. Soon enough, the wagon train faded into the distance.

"It is beautiful," said Morning Star, as she watched me stare off dreamily at our surroundings.

"God must have created this last after practicing on everything else," I said with a laugh. Indeed, lush rolling hills of grasses stretched out far as the eye could see as interrupted by stands of cottonwood, pine, fir, and aspen, and divided by rivers and streams. Topping the scene off in the background was the Laramie Range still capped at the very top with snow.

"We go build ranch?" teased Morning Star.

I put my heels to Paint's sides and lurched out in front of my warrior wife. "What are you waiting for?"

Chapter 10

First Ranch

We stopped for the night beside the North Platte River at a spot I'd visited before on a hunt. It was a peaceful spot well-sheltered from passersby. Willows arched toward the life-giving waters. In no time at all, we had a small cooking fire going. Morning Star caught a trout that would soon serve as dinner, along with some wild berries.

"Soon, we will enjoy Running Waters' cooking," I teased.

"I cook good," pouted Morning Star.

"Yes, you do," I chuckled, as I watched her skewer the trout for roasting over the fire.

We enjoyed as fine a final trail meal as ever and soon found ourselves laying atop our bedroll with our saddles as pillows. Afore long, stars began to emerge across the night sky. Morning Star nestled closely, my arm around her shoulders.

"I am a lucky man," I said softly.

"Why you lucky?" she asked.

"Tathanka captured me, and it led me to you," I explained.

"That not luck, Isa. It be work of God."

I stroked her hair as it fell freely over her shoulders and nearly to her waist. "God is good," I agreed.

"Awentia have child," she disclosed with a loving tone to her sweet voice.

"Someday, we will have children," I assured her. I'd quite obviously missed what she was telling me.

She shook her head gently. "We have child soon," she announced quite definitively.

I gave her a curious look.

"Awentia no bleed," she shared with a tentative look while searching my eyes.

My eyes opened wide and jaw dropped just a tad. My warrior woman was with child. I scooped her into my arms. "This is wonderful!" I declared. My mind raced with all that lay ahead.

"We must build home," Morning Star cooed. "Must have warm home for family." With that, she reached up and kissed me with passion.

* * *

There was now a new sense of purpose to our homeward travel. We couldn't wait to share the news with George and Running Waters. Morning Star was anxious to get word to her aging father, Spotted Elk. Our excitement must have somehow been transmitted to Paint and the mare, as they exhibited renewed energy despite enduring so many weeks of our escape from Bull Elk and our adventures in Yellowstone National Park. As to Taabe and the pack, they too showed extra vigor as they accompanied us.

We waved at some folks availing themselves of the Emigrant's Wash Tub, as we rode by without stopping. We were so close to home that we'd arrive in time for dinner.

As the Circled Cross Ranch buildings came into view, we stopped and dismounted along the south bank of the North Platte River to gather our wits. We took a long gander at each other. We were a mess to look at. There's just so much that youth and good looks can compensate for. Our buckskins were a torn and dirty mess, and I'd managed to grow a few whiskers on my young chin. Worst of all, we pretty much stunk to high heaven.

"Are you thinking what I'm thinking?" I asked Morning Star as I pinched my nose.

She laughed and grabbed my hand. A moment later, we were soaking wet in the refreshingly clear waters of the river. We tossed water at each other, and she managed to dunk me. I returned that favor with relish. We were having a great time of it.

"What are you kids up to?" came a familiar voice.

Waist-deep in water, we looked up to see George and his big, beautiful smile. "Er, we're bathing," I said, as though we'd hardly been away.

George was off his cayuse and wading into the water to hug us before we could make it to shore. "Praise the Lord, it's wonderful to see you. We were worried sick about that rogue Cheyenne Bull Elk."

We all managed to slosh hand-in-hand to the riverbank through the rushing waters.

"We reckoned to clean up for y'all," I chided.

"Well, time's a-wasting, let's get you two on down to the house. You can clean up and get ready for dinner. We're all anxious to hear of your adventures." George mounted up, then paused to take a long gander at Morning Star.

She offered a blushing smile.

George's gaze shifted knowingly to me.

I nodded.

"Yeehaw!" he hollered and spurred his horse to a gallop.

We wrung ourselves out just a tad, mounted up, and followed along in George's dust. Even the warm mountain air rushing against us as we galloped the nearly two miles to the ranch house wasn't enough to dry us out. Galloping might be an exaggeration, as Paint and the mare weren't up to more than a fast trot, not quite a canter. We arrived clean but still grungy.

George alerted everyone to our arrival. So it was that we pulled up to a throng of joyful faces. Running Waters, Esmeralda, Hap, and Dred joined George, whooping and hollering at our return.

Running Waters ignored our damp clothes and hugged us warmly. "We are so happy that you are safe. We worry for you."

Hap and Dred came up and slapped me on the back. "Dang, but yuh growed a tad," observed Hap.

"Ah thinks he be tryin' to grow whiskers," laughed Dred.

I blushed at their good-natured observations.

Running Waters laid her eyes long and lovingly upon Morning Star. "It is true," she said.

Morning Star nodded.

George stepped up. "We found some clean clothes for you. Dinner's in about an hour, so y'all have time to clean up. We can hardly wait to hear of your travels."

* * *

Dinner was mostly spent talking about the goings-on at Circled Cross Ranch while we were away. Tension built toward an after-dinner fireside chat about our adventures.

Daresay, we didn't disappoint everyone. We described our escape from the burning cabin, the help from Tathanka and the Lakota, meeting Wally the old mountain man, and dealing with bears and Indians. We described Bull Elk's demise as best we could. George interjected that the Cheyenne Chief Dull Knife would be pleased. We spent most of the discussion describing Yellowstone National Park as glowingly inspiring as possible within the limitations of words.

"How did it compare to Palo Duro Canyon?" asked George.

"There is no comparing," I said. "They are two very different places. Each holds wonders for the eyes. I think Yellowstone has more of a mystical feel."

"I have not seen this Palo Duro place...yet," contributed Morning Star. The implication wasn't missed.

"Y'all planning to visit Texas?" asked George, responding to the hint.

Morning Star and I looked at each other. "We figure to live in both places," I revealed. "Raise horses up here and beeves down there."

"That's ambitious as all get out," observed Dred. "Why not do both up here?"

"Horse no need so much land," said Morning Star.

George nodded his agreement with the truth of that. "Truth is, y'all figure to avoid the Wyoming winter," he said with a wry grin.

I laughed. "That's part of it. I also want our children to know their Texas family."

"That good," observed Running Waters. "That very good." She nodded heartfelt agreement at the wisdom of our plan.

The long day finally caught up with Morning Star and me. Running Waters had prepared a space in one of two rooms that had been added to their cabin. Their ranch had increasingly been serving as a place to repair wagons and trade for necessities, so the expansion had been important to maintain an element of privacy. We crawled into the soft bedding and soon fell asleep.

* * *

Life sure was turning out good. Morning Star was fast asleep, and I found myself restless at the prospect of heading out in the morning to look over the land that would be our first ranch. I noiselessly eased her arm from my shoulder, climbed from our bed, and wandered out under the night sky. A silvery moon soared above me, lending its shimmering light to the surrounding prairie. I had a nearly overwhelming feeling of peace. My soul seemed to be in a good place. This Wyoming, this crown on God's creation, called me to its bosom. I gazed at a close-by stand of aspens. Their leaves fluttered like jewels in the soft late summer breeze. Had it not been for my vision quest and my fortuitous meeting with Morning Star at the hands of my Lakota captors, I might yet be a young teen aimlessly wandering the vast reaches of the mountains and plains of this beautiful western paradise.

Grass and water were abundant. The twenty-five head of cattle my pa had gifted us had grazed heartily while Morning Star and I were on our journey. But it was horses that I wanted to raise. I reckoned I could trade cattle for breeding stock. I'd heard of the Quarter Horse and figured to breed the very best.

A pair of blue eyes framed in long gray fur drew up beside me. Taabe nuzzled me out of my dream. A lavender haze was signaling the sun's arrival on the eastern horizon. Another hour or so, and George, Morning Star, and I would be mounting up and looking for the perfect place to build our new home.

Homesteading had begun to gather steam in Wyoming, especially south of us toward Cheyenne, where trains of the Union Pacific Railroad chugged through. We weren't looking for any more than the minimum claim of 160 acres just yet. To qualify, the homesteader had to be a US citizen, never borne arms against the US government, and either be twenty-one years old or head of a family. Well, we were at present a family of two with a third on the way. To own the land, we had to live on and improve it for five years. As far as we could figure, there should be no problem. We'd pick our land and go file a claim.

I strode through the front door of George's house and was met by the aromatic smell of fresh-brewed coffee. Morning Star, Running Waters, and Esmeralda were busy cooking up breakfast. The mixture of aromas was so heavenly as to just about make me light-headed.

"Where have you been?" asked Running Waters.

Morning Star just gave me a winsome smile, as she'd seen me leave our bed early and sensed what I was up to.

"Just out borrowing some Wyoming air," I said jokingly. I sidled over to Morning Star and kissed her cheek. "Big day ahead," I added.

* * *

We rode out after breakfast with George in the lead. He was convinced that he'd found the perfect spot to establish our ranch. It was a tad south of his spread and situated along the Laramie River well west of Fort Laramie. He reckoned we'd have access to plenty of water for livestock, and the terrain was flatter than most in the region.

We'd ridden for a little better than an hour along the north bank of the river, when George pulled up. "There," he said with a sweeping motion of his hand. "There it sits." He laid his characteristic broad smile on us.

Morning Star and I looked at each other with hesitant nods.

"Let's cross the river and look more closely," I suggested. My eyes were sweeping the landscape for high ground and stands of trees that would lend themselves to self-defense. I wasn't figuring us to end up like the burned-out homesteaders we'd passed a few days back.

I led the way to the south shore. Well, a hundred and sixty acres is small by Texas standards. I'd heard that Texas Rangers in the mid-1800s were paid in six-hundred-acre plots. My pa already was ranching nearly a hundred thousand acres. Richard King had amassed over a million acres for his ranch in South Texas. Yep, our starter ranch here in Wyoming would be quite modest by those standards.

Our prospective homestead wouldn't be too far from the Emigrant's Wash Tub, and I reckoned that place would one day turn into a town.

We spent the next couple of hours exploring the acreage. There was a peace to be found in the abundance of the land. Stands of cottonwood and aspen would offer plenty of firewood for years to come. There was plenty of room for pasture, and the gentle rolling hills meant that we'd likely not worry overmuch about massive snowdrifts come winter storms. Morning Star rode up to what we fancied to be the highest ground and best spot to build a house. Importantly, there were plenty of rocks to be had. "Awentia love this place," she stated definitively. She dismounted. Gazing off at a stand of aspen a hundred or so yards away, she took a deep breath, kneeled, and picked a wildflower which she held beneath her nose. "This good," she said with loving eyes riveted on me.

"Let's stake it, George," I said firmly.

With our homestead site chosen, it remained to register our claim. "There's an agent over near Fort Laramie name of Clayborne Eberhart. Y'all can register your claim with him," advised George. "Once y'all own the land and assuming success, y'all can buy up adjoining properties. The Circled Cross has already grown to more than five thousand acres. Of course, the Oregon Trail slices through the northernmost part." Our Black friend paused. "Eberhart will be difficult. He hates Indians. Y'all will have the law on your side, but it won't be easy," he said by way of a warning.

With high hopes for our future, we headed back to George's spread with plans to head to Fort Laramie next morning.

* * *

The land agent's office was a ramshackle affair that had obviously been constructed with haste. It looked as though a decent storm might blow it away. Nevertheless, we knocked on its door, and a tired voice invited us to enter.

"Pardon, are you Mr. Eberhart?" I asked.

The frail, bespeckled character behind the caged service window scanned us up and down. "What be your business here, Injun?" he asked with his eyes condescendingly aimed down his long nose at us and his face giving off a flavor of considerable superiority.

"This is where homesteads are registered, isn't it?" I inquired.

"To register, y'all must be White," he stated flatly. "Go back to your reservation."

With George's warning in mind, I stayed calm. Even Morning Star didn't give off even a hint of upset. I raised my hand in front of the agent and turned it before his eyes. "Looks pretty white to me."

"Well, you're a breed, and she don't count none."

I'd dealt with a little prejudice now and again and knew that my pa made defeating it his great life purpose. George's caution still held fast with me. "I'm the son of Jack O'Toole," I replied.

"I don't give a hoot whose son you are," he responded indignantly.

"Nothing in the law says a claimant must be White," I pressed.

Eberhart guffawed so vigorously that his glasses nearly fell from his nose. "You think you're a smart Injun!" he declared behind arched eyebrows.

I reckoned this was going to be getting nastier right quickly. I'm a peace-loving man so far as possible, but I'd experienced a frontier life that few folks—especially none of Eberhart's ilk—could begin to live, much less understand. I glanced around the tiny office. I turned my head away from Eberhart and winked at Morning Star. " Awentia, do you remember the man who called you those terribly vile names?"

Morning Star caught onto my ruse quickly and

nodded with a desperate look in her eyes. "The man you scalped?" she said with a feigned gasp.

Eberhart saw her expression, heard her response, and fell into a mix of bewilderment and fear.

I saw his hand move under the counter.

Before he could grab the gun that surely resided there, I reached through the cage bars with my Bowie knife in one hand and the other grasping the collar around his sorry excuse for a neck. He found himself looking squarely at the tip of my blade. "You are a revolting excuse for a human being, Mr. Eberhart." I laid a steely gaze upon him. "I've served Colonel Stanley and Lieutenant Colonel George Custer on the Yellowstone Expedition. I'm looking to stake a claim to land to help build this territory. How dare you refuse us!" My knife edge now hovered at his throat.

"B-b-but..." he stuttered.

"There are no *buts* here, Mr. Eberhart." I handed him the description of our claim. "Our good friend George Freeman assured us that we'd have no problem. Was he speaking truthfully?"

"G-G-George?" echoed Eberhart as though he feared our friend more than my blade.

I nodded. "Now, if you're ready to proceed with registering our claim, I'd be happy to take this knife away from your throat."

Eberhart nodded so far as the proximity of my knife permitted and swiftly placed both hands on the counter.

"Wonderful. I'll put my knife away, and you can do the job the government pays you to do." I detested resorting to a threat, but Eberhart left me no choice. It was by the grace of God that I had persuaded him. Would I have cut his throat? The click of his revolver hammer being pulled back might not have ended well for the man.

Eberhart wiped beads of sweat from his forehead as he proceeded to perform his sworn duties. He soon shoved an official-looking paper across the counter at us. "P-p-please tell George that I gave y'all no trouble."

It amused me that Eberhart was prejudiced against Indians but held a Black man in obvious respect. "I'll be sure to tell him, Mr. Eberhart," I responded.

As we strode from the shack with our land grant in hand, Morning Star turned to me. "Would Isa cut man's throat?"

I stopped mid-stride and looked down at her. "Maybe cut him just a little," I said, pinching my fingers together and offering a grin.

She smiled. "God pleased."

We headed for George's ranch.

* * *

With our homestead claim registered, now came the job of actually building our house. George loaned us Hap and Dred to help. Once we laid out the corners of the foundation, we could begin the task of leveling the ground and laying footings along with a stone floor. The toughest work was finding and hauling rocks for the floor and walls. There were plenty of them to be found, but finding the right sizes and then fitting them offered a constant challenge. We used a technique called dry stacking, whereby stones were fit as precisely as possible.

It would have taken a couple of weeks to obtain windows, but we were fortunate to encounter a trader at Fort Laramie who just happened to have four that he was pleased to trade to us in exchange for a horse. I think the trader got a bargain. I recalled my pa telling me how the famed Lewis and Clark Expedition valued horses so much that they'd trade weapons for them. Transportation was of primary concern as the expedition wound its way up the Missouri River. Dealing with the trader did give me the opportunity to let him know of my plans to breed horses. Traders tended to cover a lot of territory, so word would get out.

"Buildin' a far-sized place here, Isa," observed Hap. "Gonna last forever," he added, referring to the stone construction.

I stood, wiped my brow, and surveyed our construction progress. "Surely hope so."

"Whatcha putting on the roof?" asked Dred.

Given that our original cabin with log walls and thatched roof had burned down, we had given serious thought to fireproofing so much as possible. "I reckon to make it impossible for the house to burn down. That fellow I traded with for the windows is coming back next month with clay tiles."

"They might smoke yuh out," surmised Hap.

I offered a broad smile. "Got that licked, Hap."

Dred and Hap paused from hefting rocks to hear what I had in mind. "We're going to branch the flue."

"Huh?" exclaimed Hap.

Morning Star sidled over to me. She had been working on squaring and smoothing the massive piece of wood that would serve as a mantel over our hearth. She'd been listening to our conversation. "Smithy at Fort Laramie make special flue. If top of chimney blocked, we pull lever to open second flue. It sends smoke outside from side of chimney."

I nodded, as Morning Star nailed the description. It

was an ingenious contraption that I reckoned the smithy should protect legally. It sure enough impressed Hap and Dred.

Dred shook his head admiringly. "Y'all be buildin' more fort than house."

"That's what my pa did down in Texas," I recalled. "Frustrated the dickens out of the Indians."

"Bein' an Injun, expect y'all know how they be thinkin'," observed Hap.

From anyone other than Hap, Morning Star and I might have been offended. He was right. We knew the tactics the Indians used to attack homesteads. Our living spaces, while comfortable, anticipated their tactics and featured appropriate defenses. "Pretty much, Hap." I gazed thoughtfully at the two cowpokes. "If rumors are true, the tribes will gather together soon to fight the Whites. Meanwhile, many homesteads will be attacked."

"Do yuh think the Circled Cross Ranch will be safe?" asked Dred.

"George has built it about as safe as can be expected. He's got pretty fair relations with the tribes. Besides..."

"Whatcha mean *besides*?" echoed Hap.

I laughed. "Well, for one thing, George isn't a White man."

"Hap and Dred must worry," chided Morning Star with a mischievous laugh.

The two cowboys stared aghast at each other.

"She's joking with you," I assured them. "Y'all will be about as safe as can be at the Circled Cross Ranch."

With nervous chuckles, Hap and Dred shrugged and returned to fitting rocks into the walls.

There was one more thing we did that was aimed at frustrating any enemy. We dug a well inside the walls. We could hold off an enemy for weeks, if necessary.

By the end of October, we'd placed the final tiles on the roof and made the interior homey. Morning Star had even pulled me in to help with interior decoration. Her *woman's touch* was colored by living in a teepee as a Lakota. She drew upon my experience growing up in a house with four walls. Our stone house afforded space unlike any she'd previously encountered. It was three times the size of the log cabin we'd initially lived in.

One of the great fortunes of living near the Oregon Trail was our access to furniture that pioneers had discarded on their way west. As the mountains loomed ahead, many realized that the load they carried in their prairie schooners was simply far too heavy. Precious heirloom furniture was often set by the side of the trail. As a consequence, we were able to outfit our cabin with beautiful furniture. The fine workmanship offered a stark contrast to the rock walls and rough-hewn timbers within our house. Morning Star especially treasured a rig called a dressing table featuring an ornately framed mirror.

I enjoyed watching Morning Star gracefully comb her hair while seated before the mirror. Then she would stand and look at her protruding belly. She'd turn to me and smile. These were happy days.

* * *

Hap, Dred, and the Freemans were also generous in helping to furnish our home. Tableware and cooking utensils seemed to magically appear. Running waters had even kept the cradleboard from the foundling Lakota baby they'd adopted, and she gave it to us in anticipation of the birth of our first child.

We still had to build a barn and corral in anticipation

of raising Quarter Horses. With winter close at hand, there was no point in trading out my beeves for horses. We'd constructed a baffle similar to George's that would offer some protection for our cattle against winter storms. Our baffle featured a roof-like cover that extended to our house to afford sheltered access. I also reduced the size of our herd by a half dozen that I sold to Fort Laramie. We also stocked up on feed for the remaining herd. In short, we were ready for whatever storms and frigid temperatures were thrown at us. We also had plenty of food and firewood to see us comfortably through the coming cold season.

If there was a downside to all our preparation, it was that a rough winter could keep us penned up indoors for long periods. To fend off boredom, we stocked books and materials for Morning Star to undertake her decorative beadwork and to fashion new buckskins for us. I would fashion new arrows, do a bit of wood carving, be sure the livestock were faring well, and keep our guns in working order. I reckoned that boredom was the least of our worries, as we were still enjoying God's blessings on our union. Morning Star's pregnancy didn't diminish us expressing our passions. God surely had blessed us both.

Chapter 11

Winter to Remember

November kicked off with memorable greetings. I was feeding the cattle and horses right after breakfast and took a gander at the Laramie Range off to the west. Forebodingly dark clouds were gathering. These were the sort of clouds that were nearly black at their bottom with a creamy icing-like upper layer. They were rolling in fast. I hurried up with my livestock chores, only this time I didn't release them to pasture. They were none too happy, but it was for their own good.

The wind began to whip up a bit. Morning Star had lived all fifteen years of her life up here, so she was well acquainted with northern plains blizzards. I had experienced them twice last year, so I had a pretty fair idea of what to expect.

As a final preparatory task, I battened the shutters over the windows. We didn't need ice crystals or hailstones breaking the glass.

With the livestock cared for as best I could, I headed inside. "Got a norther coming," I said matter-of-factly to Morning Star. By this time, the wind was letting loose sporadic howls. The beeves could be heard bawling and bellowing, and horses let loose with nervous neighing and whinnying.

"Is a big one," observed Morning Star.

I nodded. "I'm afraid so. I hope George got back from his trip to Fort Laramie."

"What about wagon train?" Morning Star was referring to a foolhardy wagon master leading a train of ten wagons on the Oregon Trail. They had passed by just a day ago, and would surely be caught up in the heart of what would be a full-blown raging blizzard.

I dropped a couple of logs on the fire. The hearth had been built to radiate heat through the great room, including the kitchen area. We'd be toasty through most any storm. "Hopefully, they had the sense to find shelter," I replied to Morning Star's concern. "Even at that, they'll be lucky to survive," I lamented.

We'd watched as the train ambled past far to the north of our house. I was certain that George would have advised them against continuing, and they'd have received the same advice from Fort Laramie. I suspected they'd avoided the fort for fear that the soldiers would have forced them to make camp nearby for the winter. I dreaded to imagine what we'd find once this storm passed. The mournful howling of the wind had begun to turn to raging roars. Ice began to ricochet off the stone walls and shutters. This was fixing to be the nastiest of storms. I dreaded to think what God might have in store for us when winter fully set in.

I watched Morning Star as she prepared a piping-hot venison stew. Its stick-to-the-ribs goodness was exactly what I was ready for. I couldn't help but notice that her belly had begun to offer visual proof of the child we were expecting. It led me to wonder how my pa had reacted to my ma's first pregnancy. Running Waters had guessed that the baby would come into this world at the very beginning of spring.

* * *

Well, that blizzard raged for two solid days. When the winds had fully simmered down, we donned our furs and opened the front door to a veritable winter wonderland. The sun's rays beneath a crystal-clear azure sky revealed a bejeweled landscape fit for royalty. We stepped out tentatively at first. Given that our house was built atop a rise in the sprawling plains, the snow wasn't deep around us. We were confident that any ravines and crevices would be packed with drifted snowfall.

"Let's check on the livestock," I urged.

Morning Star nodded, and we headed for the livestock shelter.

The best news was that the temperatures weren't below freezing. It was still a tad too early in the season for sustained frigidity. The cattle and horses moved about at our approach and welcomed our feeding them. We gave Paint and Morning Star's mare special sugar treats which were much appreciated. The beeves had pretty much trampled any snow into near oblivion. We patted each animal as much to calm them as to keep them reminded of the care they received from their human handlers.

My gaze swept to beneath where the baffle cover met the house. There lay Taabe and his pack, enjoying the remains of a fresh deer kill. Alerted to our presence, Taabe padded on over and put a cold, wet nose to my cheek. He repeated the greeting with Morning Star.

"Are you thinking what I'm thinking?" I asked Morning Star.

"Look for wagon train?" she replied.

I nodded. "Likely a foolhardy idea, but I have a feeling they're in big trouble." It seemed like the neighborly thing to do, even if the neighbors were just passing through.

"Maybe visit George first. Hap and Dred help."

What she was suggesting made sense. There was no point in finding the wagon train and being short on the help needed to render assistance.

We bundled up, saddled up, and headed for the Circled Cross Ranch.

* * *

Even with the small amount of snow, it took a couple of hours to wend our way across terrain featuring crevices covered with snow or slippery ice-coated rocks. We often walked Paint and the mare to avoid treacherous places.

It was late morning, when we finally reached George's house. He must have seen us coming, as he opened the front door as we arrived. "Welcome!" he called. "Y'all getting cabin fever?" When we didn't dismount, he had a clue that we were up to more.

"We were wondering how that wagon train made out in the blizzard," shared Morning Star.

George shook his head. "I was curious myself. I advised the fool of a wagon master that he was headed for trouble."

"We were wondering whether you, Hap, and Dred might be up to joining us to see whether they needed help. They sure couldn't have gotten far in two days of travel plus hunkering down for the blizzard," I proposed.

George rubbed his chin thoughtfully for a moment.

Running Waters poked her head out. "Come have coffee while George gets wagon," she invited while giving her now-smiling husband his marching orders.

We dismounted.

George went off to roust Hap and Dred.

Only a half-hour later, we were traipsing westward on the Oregon Trail. Given that we could travel faster than the lumbering prairie schooners used by the settlers, we reckoned that we'd reach the wagon train a tad before nightfall.

Our journey was uneventful. We passed a small Crow encampment well off to the north of our path and could see children playing in the snow under the watchful eyes of their mothers. There was a feeling of life returning to normal despite a temperature hovering around freezing. Plenty of game emerged from time to time from stands of juniper and aspen to forage in the encrusted snow.

We had judged about right as to when we'd reach the wagon train. It was a sorry sight to the eye. They had chosen a poor spot to shelter. The conditions were bleak, as snowdrifts had piled up against the wagons. There was nary a fire to be seen, as families huddled for warmth under blankets inside the wagons. Livestock looked about ready to collapse from exhaustion, hunger, and the cold. We expected the wagon master to come out to greet us, but he was nowhere to be found.

Hap and Dred went about gathering wood and building a fire that was soon throwing its warmth within the circle of wagons. The two cowhands quickly placed iron pots on the fire filled with a stew that Running Waters had quickly pulled together back at the ranch.

George, Morning Star, and I began checking on the wagons, urging folks to come out, get warm, and enjoy warm drinks and the stew.

"Wh-wh-where you from?" stuttered a woman through near-frozen lips.

"Just nearby ranchers. Saw y'all pass through the other day and took to worrying about you with the blizzard and all," I responded.

The look in her eyes, when she realized she was talking with a half-breed, a Lakota woman, and a Black man, seemed to unsettle her slightly. "You are a blessing," she finally said as she headed for the warmth of the fire.

"Where's the wagon master?" George asked, as she staggered past.

She paused with a sad expression, shrugged, and moved on.

We became aware that there were no men around. Well, there was one, but he was an old man with frail faculties. Why would the men abandon the wagons?

We ensured that all folks in the wagons were now gathered around the fire and enjoying that big batch of stew. There were nine grown women and twenty children so far as we could determine. "Where are the men?" I asked the woman we'd encountered earlier.

"Gone. Seek food and better campsite." Her response didn't totally make sense. Why would the men totally abandon the women, leaving them to the harsh elements? Wasn't there food in the wagons? Even in cold weather, the unguarded wagon train was an easy target for hostile Indians looking for scalps and the coveted supplies in the wagons.

Morning Star and I stepped aside with George, while Hap and Dred cared for the women and children as best they could. Frostbite wasn't a problem, though they were bone-chillingly cold. "What do you think, George?" I asked. "Escort them back to Fort Laramie?" I recognized that it would entail three days of travel in the cold weather for these already weakened travelers.

"We have no choice," contributed Morning Star. "They cannot go on."

We still had to deal with the question of what had become of the men? Winds had been sufficient to blow away any tracks in the snow. Perhaps they had gotten too far from the wagon train and had lost their bearings. Hap and Dred went about preparing the wagons to head back to Fort Laramie. It took a lot of coaxing to get the oxen to respond, but they were managing the job.

I decided to scout the periphery of the circle of wagons in hopes of finding some faint sign. I was about a hundred yards out to the west of the wagons and near the south bank of the North Platte River when I came upon a glove. I waved to Morning Star and George to join me. They took a couple of horses from the wagon train remuda just in case we found the men and needed extra transportation.

"Why would someone drop a glove and not retrieve it?" I asked sort of rhetorically.

"Something's gone terribly wrong," added George.

Morning Star had ridden a few paces west of us. "Here another glove," she stated.

It was looking like someone was freeing their hands to use a rifle. The three of us headed in the direction we surmised that the men had headed. We'd gone about a mile, when we reached ground from which the snow had blown away or begun to melt.

"Look!" I exclaimed, pointing to a couple of boot prints.

Morning Star assessed the prints more closely. "Man

run," she observed, as she noted that the impression of the toe was far deeper than the heel and the stride was longer than that of a walk.

My own tracking skills came into play. The trail was alternately icy, muddy, and rocky. It was treacherous in spots. Fortunately, we didn't have to travel far, perhaps a mile at most. We passed a stand of aspen and came upon a horrific scene. Bodies were strewn all over the landscape. Some had been shot while others featured multiple arrows in their bodies. All had been scalped.

"Cheyenne!" gasped Morning Star.

I nodded. "These men must have run head-on into a hunting party with a grudge." The bodies were frozen in various states of pain and agony. A couple had obviously been scalped while still alive. The Cheyenne were long gone, so we dismounted. The deathly silence was broken only by a stiff breeze whistling among the trees. There was an eeriness about the place. But hours earlier, these had been living, breathing human beings.

As I bent to check on the first body we approached, we heard a muffled groan from the direction of the aspens. I scanned the trees, and deciding it was safe, headed cautiously toward the sound.

"H-h-help…" came the moaning call.

I found a young man—no older than fourteen or fifteen—hiding behind a tree. He's dug himself in such that he was nearly covered in snow. The teen had caught two arrows, one in his upper leg and a second in his upper arm. He was in considerable pain and had done a bit of bleeding.

When he saw me with my long dark hair and high Comanche cheekbones, he drew back in terror. He'd seen how the Cheyenne had scalped his companions and undoubtedly thought I was one of them. "No! No!" he cried, his unwounded arm covering the top of his head.

I smiled in an attempt to ease his fears. "Don't worry. I'm here to help," I assured him. I turned back toward the others. "George! Morning Star! This one's alive," I said with a motion to join me.

By this time, fear had caused the young man to pass out.

"He's a young one," lamented George. "Let's get him back to the wagons."

We got the teen roused from his hiding place, and despite the arrows which we decided not to remove out here in cold, managed to seat him on a horse. He nearly fainted again with the combination of pain and sight of the scalped bodies of his companions. For all we knew, his father might have been among the dead. Fortunately for the teen, the horse moved with some gentleness across the rough terrain. This made for slow going, but we wanted this survivor to live to tell us what happened.

By the time we reached the wagons, Hap and Dred had the train ready to move out. When they saw us coming, they alerted the womenfolk. A couple of them tumbled from the trailing wagons to treat our quite obviously wounded find.

"Billy!" a woman called. "What did they…?" Her question trailed off, as Billy was helped from the horse and eased into the last wagon where the arrows could be removed and his wounds treated in relative warmth. We were desperate to learn what had befallen him and the men.

Billy was still suffering from shock but tried to tell the story while the women treated his wounds. I feared that removing the arrows would cause him to pass out again, but he was anxious enough to share what had happened so as to remain lucid. "We knew a storm was coming," he began. "Wagon master led five men out to find better shelter. Didn't know Injuns was around. The wagon master was ambushed."

"Why did the others go out?" I asked.

"That storm was coming in faster than we thought. We worried about the wagon master, so we left old man Simms behind and headed out to find the others. Just as we found the bodies, we was attacked. The storm began at nearly the same time. I found shelter behind that tree where y'all found me. As the storm whipped up, I saw them Injuns scalp…" Billy's words trailed off.

I shook my head with dismay. The wagon master had been very foolish. Had he not ignored the advice from Fort Laramie and then from George, they'd all likely still be alive. As it was, there were now several widows and children without fathers in the wagon train.

"Are there bodies to be buried?" asked one of the women.

George sighed. "They're all dead, ma'am, and the ground is too frozen to bury them."

"Can we bring them to the fort?" she entreated.

Morning Star, George, and I looked at each other, then turned to Dred and Hap. "Is there room in our wagon?" The vision of stacked frozen human bodies sent a chill up my spine, but respect for the dead and the wishes of a handful of freshly made widows was surely of considerable concern. Hap and Dred nodded. We'd make room, if we had to.

"Hap, you and Dred head toward the fort. We'll go back and retrieve the…er…unfortunate souls." George tried to be delicate.

Morning Star decided to help the women. Despite

the weather conditions, she found the fixings for poultices for Billy's wounds. We were grateful that the young man had survived to tell his story.

I took a last look at the now-sleeping teen. Billy's life would be forever changed. Manhood had been thrust upon him.

George and I turned our wagon and drove it back to the scene of the massacre. Upon arrival, we were struck by how gruesome it was. The Cheyenne had taken their victims' ears along with scalps. It was as though they were venting great anger borne of frustration.

"It's not the beginning, George," I observed. "Nor is it the end. There will be worse to come."

George nodded. His trademark smile was absent.

We laid the bodies in the wagon bed as respectfully as we could under the circumstances. The temperature was dropping. With nine bodies loaded along with the iron stew kettle along with a few supplies and weapons, the wagon now had a pretty fair load to be pulled. George tied his horse to the back while I rode Paint alongside. We figured to catch up to the wagon train when it stopped for the night. I thanked God that a second storm hadn't piggybacked on the first one. That phenomenon tended to occur now and then up here in the mountains.

One of the blessings of the blizzard was that it had likely caused any Cheyenne hostiles to shelter in their teepees. We kept a watch but felt confident there would be no further attacks for the immediate future.

It took three days to reach Fort Laramie. The soldiers at the fort were actually relieved to have some women around, despite many of the new guests being widows. I guessed that it gave the unmarried men among them some sort of sense of hope for the future.

The major in command was sympathetic to the plight

of the settlers. He offered medical assistance and shared the hospitality of the US Army. The wagons were parked in a circle a couple of hundred yards from the fort, as it was important to have a clear line of sight across the surrounding terrain. In the event of any attack, there was no point in providing cover for hostile forces.

Come spring, the settlers would have to make the decision as to whether to continue westward or return to the east. With the menfolk gone, all but the hardiest of the survivors would likely give up their dreams of settling in Oregon.

* * *

It was roughly two weeks from the wagon train incident, when Morning Star and I made it back to our home. While it had lent some excitement to what otherwise might have been winter doldrums, we appreciated the good feelings we experienced in helping others.

The morning after our arrival, fresh storm clouds began to whip up on the horizon. I quickly began getting reacquainted with our livestock. Incredibly, they were all accounted for.

Who should appear now but Taabe. "Where you been?" I asked. He cocked his head as though saying, *what are you talking about?* I suppose he'd been hanging back here guarding the house and livestock.

Sure enough, another storm blew through. It didn't pack the punch of the first one, but it signaled the onslaught of winter—and it was only late November.

My idea of building our house with stone was paying off, as the interior was warm and toasty. This was wonderful, as the ongoing winter delivered more storms. Morning Star assured me that she'd endured worse cold and snow growing up in a Lakota teepee. We had snow and freezing temperatures down in Texas but nothing to compare with the northern plains and mountains.

We passed the time between chores by reading and talking out plans for growing the ranch come spring. We had a barn and corral to build and would sell most of the remaining beeves to buy breeding horses. There was decent trade in cattle, but a good horse was worth its weight in gold. There would be a significant challenge in protecting the horses from marauding Indians.

We enjoyed Christmas before a roaring fire and some wine I'd been hiding for the right occasion. It appeared that my vision quest had been achieved, if the ultimate destination had indeed been settling on a life purpose. Ranches, family, friends, and a loving wife seemed downright purposeful. If there was any more to the vision quest, God had certainly not revealed it.

We made one venture to Fort Laramie. The settlers from the wagon train that we'd saved from further Indian predations had made themselves at home around the fort. They welcomed us warmly. Billy, in particular, expressed his deep gratitude for saving him.

Colonel Stanley had returned from Fort Lincoln but was headed to Texas to deal with Indian predations. A generalship likely awaited him. "Welcome to Fort Laramie, Isa," he greeted. "Have y'all decided to settle here?" He gave me a once-over as though saying I'd grown up quite a bit since my days on his Yellowstone Expedition.

"Thank you, Colonel. We built a home on a few acres a couple of days west and just south of the Oregon Trail. We're going to raise Quarter Horses."

Stanley nodded amicably. He was quite obviously

impressed. "You ever get back to Texas, I'd welcome you as a scout."

I appreciated the colonel's offer. "Thanks, Colonel, but when we do get to Texas, it'll be to build a cattle ranch like my pa's."

"Well, it's a standing offer, Isa." He looked over at Morning Star with her ever-growing belly and nodded his understanding. "Best of luck to you, Isa. As the Mexicans down in Texas say, *Vaya con Dios*."

"Bless you, too, Colonel Stanley. Safe travels."

Morning Star was waiting for me to load the last of the supplies into our wagon. "What did blue coat want?"

I laughed at her reference to troopers as *blue coats*. Her Lakota heritage snuck through now and then. "He asked me to scout for him in Texas," I replied.

She smiled, as I helped her hoist a bag of flour into the wagon. She kissed my cheek. "We ranch, no scout."

I nodded. Morning Star was right, of course. So far as I was concerned, that was the way it would be. Besides, I didn't want to be thought of as a scout just because of my Comanche heritage.

* * *

We managed to find our way to George's place to celebrate Christmas. It was festive, especially as Esmeralda had learned to play the piano. It was out of tune, but she could carry a melody. Hap and Dred contributed with the banjo and harmonica, while George's bass and my baritone mixed with the women to raise joyful praises. We ate until we couldn't move.

Thus, Christmas was a shining star amid the white frigidity of the North Platte country. The weeks that followed would have been dreary but for the life that my pregnant warrior wife brought to our house. There was a glow about Morning Star that deepened her beauty inside and out.

Chapter 12

Thievin' Injuns

Mid-February rolled around, throwing a couple of modest snowstorms at us. Game struggled to find food in the deep snowdrifts, and those—whether White man or Red man—who failed to adequately stock plenty of food and firewood, began dealing with the resulting deprivations. We were grateful to have had the foresight to endure what turned out to be a colder and snowier winter than what was deemed normal for the region.

I arose early one morning. I did my usual stoking of the coals in our fireplace, added a couple of logs, and soon had the house toasty warm. I even began the morning coffee brewing ritual. Morning Star crawled from under the blankets and slipped into a cotton dress that draped comfortably over her growing belly. We'd be indoors this day, save for my checking on our livestock.

Sipping my coffee, I scraped frost from a front window and peered out across the snowy landscape. There'd been a light snowfall. Far off toward the Laramie Range, I saw a column of smoke spiraling to the sky. It was too much to have been from a campfire. I turned to

Morning Star. "Looks like the Reynolds place has been attacked," I said with a resigned calm that surprised me.

Morning Star paused from cooking. "They come soon," she replied.

I promised myself to clean and load our carbines after breakfast. Breakfast? Not many folks around these parts in mid-winter enjoyed steak, eggs, and biscuits. Morning Star even broke out some bear sign that she'd baked the day before. If we kept this up, we'd both be too fat to work the ranch come spring.

It was only two days later, when I strode out into a cold morning in my buffalo coat to lay some beef bones out for Taabe and his pack. I felt a tingling that told me that something wasn't right. I looked up to our roof and saw a Cheyenne warrior aiming an arrow at me. His hair hung in frosted wisps down his cheeks, and his eyes spoke of desperation-driven hunger. In my peripheral vision, I spotted at least three more hostiles. I'd left my carbine leaning against a nearby corral post. The savage's arrow was no more than ten feet from me. He couldn't miss.

He drew back his bowstring. I saw Taabe silently appear behind the savage. In the next instant, the bow and arrow flew off harmlessly, and the Cheyenne thudded at my feet with Taabe's jaws cracking the bones in his neck. Roughly a hundred and seventy-five pounds of wolf had been no match for the Cheyenne warrior. The warrior's three companions were horrified at the sight. They began to run, slipping and falling several times on icy spots as they scrambled in panic from my strong *sunipu*.

Morning Star had heard the commotion and appeared in the doorway. She saw Taabe gnawing away on the neck of the Cheyenne warrior, who soon went lifeless.

I was outwardly calm, but my heart was racing inside my chest. "Taabe saved my life," I stated the obvious. I turned to my wolf friend. "Taabe! No more!"

Taabe reluctantly released his grip. Mua and the other wolves appeared. All looked at me with anticipation.

Fate intervened. Two deer appeared near the baffle we'd built to protect the livestock. They stared with fear-laden eyes at Morning Star and me and then at the wolves as though accepting of their bleak destiny. Taabe and his pack wasted no time.

Now, we were left with the body of the dead Cheyenne. No matter what might have driven him to his deadly purpose, we felt a call to respect the dead. "How far to the Cheyenne village?" I asked.

Morning Star thought a moment. "What Isa do?" she asked.

"We're taking this warrior to his people and giving them one of our cattle," I replied.

"Is danger," she observed, then smiled. "But good."

* * *

We had a rough idea where the band of Cheyenne were wintering. It was a small village of no more than fifty people, as the tribe had been decimated by disease, failed encounters with soldiers, and attacks from Crow and Lakota. The encampment was near a sheltered hillside overlook facing a wide valley that was generally spared the drifting snow. It was about a half day from Morning

Star's Miniconjou Lakota people and a solid two-day ride from our homestead.

Morning Star loaded some foodstuffs, especially vegetables, onto a packhorse, while I cut two cattle from our herd. I hoisted the Cheyenne warrior's body on a second horse. We figured to head west on the Oregon Trail for a day, then cut northward to the place we thought the Cheyenne were camped.

While there was the risk of attack from hostiles, the greater risk was the weather. We packed shelter and sufficient food to endure most any storm, but winter demanded the utmost respect. It also wasn't lost on us that Morning Star was nearly seven months along in her pregnancy. She was strong, still my warrior woman wife, but what if our timing for the birthing was off? We had a decidedly arduous journey ahead. Negotiating the mountains, valleys, and rolling hills of our Yellowstone odyssey was as nothing compared to this adventure.

As we prepared to depart, I took a ride around our homestead to be sure all was secure. Satisfied, I shared a brief prayer for our success and safe return. I pushed my heels into Paint's flanks to urge him on. He looked back at me as though I was crazy. With a snort, he finally moved forward.

There we were, Morning Star and me in our saddles bundled against the cold, two trailing pack horses, two cattle, and a pack of wolves all trudging along through the trappings of winter on the northern plains. Yep, our little caravan made for quite a sight, as we trudged along valiantly against the elements. It figured that we'd be headed into a chill wind that began to grow stronger as our journey progressed. I ignored what it might portend.

We had a perfect place in mind to spend our first night on the trail. It would offer adequate shelter for our entire entourage. For a while, I wasn't so sure we'd get there while daylight lasted. Occasional drifted snow and icy places slowed our pace, and the wind blasting against us was no help. The two beeves we were gifting to the starving Cheyenne moved slowly as though sensing their fate. The cattle served to set our pace.

The sun was just about to dip behind the distant mountain, when we came upon our planned campsite. What were the odds that the place would be occupied? What were the chances that it would be occupied by none other than our old friend Wally?

"Wagh!" called Wally upon seeing us approach.

Morning Star and I gave each other an *oh no, it can't be* look.

"Come on in. The fire is right warm," invited our old mountain man friend.

We dismounted and led in the packhorses and beeves. "What brings you to this neck of the woods?" I asked.

Wally guffawed. "Reckoned to head south where it be warmer," he laughed. "Come now. Make yerselves at home."

With Wally's two mules added to the livestock, the shelter was cozy. It was a natural shelter carved by nature into a solid granite wall. As we moved into the campsite, the wind howled a warning. "Looks like we got here in the nick of time," I observed.

"Yep. Y'all figgered 'bout right," noted Wally. "Gonna hit hard an' quick," he predicted. The wind delivered another roar as though punctuating Wally's prediction.

Soon, ice pellets began ricocheting off the surrounding rocks. The campfire roared its resistance as icy bullets died with a sizzle in its flames. We ate a stick-to-the-ribs dinner topped with Wally's coffee, threw lobs on the fire, and huddled close to endure the blizzard. Taabe and his pack lay closely around us, adding the warmth of their bodies to what our blankets and the fire offered.

"This be the good Lord's doing," Wally opined.

"Think so?" asked Morning Star with a laugh.

"He at least saw fit to prepare us for it," I added. "We helped out a snow-bound wagon train a few weeks back. They hadn't been so lucky. Most all the menfolk died at the hands of hostile Cheyenne, and the women were left to deal with the storm."

"Might have turned out like the Donner party many years back," said Wally.

"Donner?" asked Morning Star.

"Yep. Back in the 1840s, they was trapped by snow in a place called the Sierra Nevada. It's said they ate the livestock and then, as members died, they ate their fellow travelers."

Morning Star was aghast.

Having heard my pa speak of the cannibalistic habits of some tribes in Texas, I was less shocked by Wally's story. "Well, this wagon train was facing hostile Cheyenne," I said by way of changing the subject.

"Cheyenne, you say?" asked Wally. "They be camped back yonder a way. What in tarnation you be thinkin'?"

Morning Star smiled and looked admiringly at me. "We go to Cheyenne. They need food."

"They burned a place near us a couple of days back. Yesterday, a small band attacked us. Taabe here saved my life by killing one who was about to shoot me at point-blank range. These people are desperate, and we reckon to make peace by bringing them food and returning the dead warrior."

Wally stared into the flames for a few minutes while

mulling over what I'd just shared. "Humph! You sure be offerin' somethin' they don't git from White folk. Mebbe, it'll work."

The blizzard whipped up its fury a bit more, as its winds wailed their song up the valley. "Might as well turn in," I suggested. "The blizzard might blow itself out by morning."

With that, I placed a couple of more logs on the fire, and we nestled in at the back of our shelter. A couple of the wolves actually took to Wally enough to snuggle with him. Only the horses, mules, and the dead Cheyenne missed out on the sharing of warm bodies.

* * *

As I'd predicted, the morning sun revealed that the storm had passed. Wally was already up and stoking the fire under the coffee pot. The alluring aroma of coffee mixed with woodsmoke served to enhance the coziness of our shelter.

Morning Star had just begun to stir. She was sleeping a tad longer these days.

Wally squinted over his shoulder at me. "Y'all still hankerin' to chase down them Cheyenne?"

I nodded, as I pulled on my high-top moccasins. "It's the right thing to do."

"The right thang might git yuh kilt," he warned.

"The wrong thing got yonder Cheyenne killed," I said while pointing to the body draped over the packhorse.

"Mind if I tag along?" asked Wally.

"Wally know Cheyenne?" queried Morning Star.

Wally chuckled and began to pour coffee. "Been frenly an' not so frenly," he said. "I speak their tongue."

Morning Star and I exchanged looks. She nodded.

"Happy to have you join us, Wally," I invited.

"Well, times a-wastin'. Let's be eatin' up an' git goin'."

I gazed out at the wintery panoply before us. Trading the warm comfort of our shelter for the frigid temperatures of the crystalline landscape before us was necessary. I guess God wanted mankind to more fully appreciate his creation by offering extremes. I'd already begun appreciating our plan to spend warmer seasons up here in the North Platte country and colder ones in Texas.

We were soon caravaning our way to where we figured the Cheyenne encampment to be. Last night's blizzard made for slightly slower going. With any luck, the Cheyenne would find us before we could find them. It would save a lot of searching, though it would likely entail a bit of parleying.

* * *

Around mid-afternoon, we found ourselves on a game trail heading along a steep hillside through stands of aspen that eventually led to juniper and pine as we journeyed higher. I reckoned it wouldn't be long before the weather would give enough hint of spring for the aspens and cottonwoods to bud. I was out front with Morning Star behind me and Wally a few paces behind our two head of cattle and our packhorses. Taabe and his pack traveled on higher ground parallel to us.

Upon rounding a bend in the trail, I found our path blocked by three mounted Cheyenne warriors. They were a fearsome trio, wrapped in fur from head to foot but bristling with weapons. They looked to be a hunting party, though the great question was what prey were they hunting?

They were about to make an aggressive grab for their weapons when they spotted Taabe on higher ground off to my left. They looked from me to the wolf and apparently made the connection that three of their fellow warriors must have described of the man with the strong medicine. One urged his pony a few steps ahead of the others and nervously made a sign for peace.

I smiled and also gave the sign for peace.

Wally moved up alongside me with mule in tow. "We come with food for Cheyenne," he said in their language.

The warrior nodded. He said something to his companions, and the three warriors turned their ponies and motioned us to follow them.

The Cheyenne encampment turned out to be about two miles from the spot we'd encountered the warriors. Smoke arose from what looked to be as many as thirty teepees.

As our procession approached, our escorts called out. Women and children began emerging from their teepees. They were a sorry-looking lot. The winter had been unkind. We endured curious stares as we rode through the encampment. Others looked amazed at Taabe and the wolves. We soon found ourselves facing the apparent chief of this band.

"That be Little Wolf," said Wally as an aside. "This be interestin'."

I had no idea what *interesting* meant.

Wally dismounted from his mule. He and the chief stared at each other for several increasingly uncomfortable moments. I had been told that Little Wolf had been one of the chiefs who signed the Fort Laramie Treaty back in 1868. He'd been none too happy about how quickly it had been broken.

Little Wolf's eyes flashed with a combination of

emotions that I wasn't able to read. Fear wasn't among them. He motioned to the three warriors who'd escorted us to join him.

"My friends bring gifts for Cheyenne," offered Wally. "This Isa of Comanche and Awentia, daughter to Wapitiyu Okle of Miniconjou Lakota."

Little Wolf's expression flashed with a hint of recognition at Spotted Elk's name. "Lakota friends with Dull Knife."

At Morning Star's urging, I stepped forward beside Wally. I had grabbed the tether of the packhorse with the body of the dead Cheyenne warrior. I expect that I made for quite a sight. A tall half-breed youth with a dead warrior in tow wasn't a common sight. I glanced at Wally. "Translate for me, please, Wally." This was my expedition, after all.

He turned to the chief. "Isa strong medicine."

I took on a serious but compassionate facial expression. "Cheyenne attack three days ago. We kill one. Others run." I was looking to establish the strength of my medicine. "We know Cheyenne hungry. We bring food and body of dead Cheyenne warrior."

Wally rattled off something in the Cheyenne tongue that I prayed was an accurate translation. "I left out the part 'bout them runnin'," he said as an aside to me. "Don't wanna call 'em cowards."

Morning Star led the two cattle forward along with a large bag of dried vegetables and flour.

Little Wolf stood for a few seconds as though cogitating on the situation. Finally, he turned to me. "You strong medicine," he observed. "You brave to come to Cheyenne camp. Isa honor Cheyenne dead."

As though on cue, Taabe walked up, sat beside me, and nuzzled my hand.

Little Wolf fought to keep his jaw from dropping. Seeing a huge Timberwolf behave in this manner was huge medicine. The chief took a deep breath and began, "Cheyenne grateful. Isa strong. Friend to Cheyenne." He scanned the gathered throng of his people. "We eat," he finally said with a broad smile.

The Cheyenne women went to work butchering the cattle, and we joined in the ensuing feast. We'd just have soon not eaten, as these people needed the food and we were well fed. A couple of head of cattle wasn't going to do a lot toward feeding more than a hundred hungry people, but I hoped it would give the warriors the energy and inclination to prey on animals rather than humans.

During the meal, Wally worked extra hard translating conversation between me and Little Wolf. The chief was especially struck by my name translating to wolf in the Comanche language. I think that little coincidence brought us together. I did share with him what I knew of the Comanche experiences with the White man's reservations, noting that conditions there could be pretty bad. Any success of reservation life would be up to the tribes themselves, as the government was of little or no help. I think Little Wolf appreciated my honest assessment, and this further established a bond of mutual trust.

When we'd finished eating, Little Wolf invited us to spend the night. With dusk approaching, he was genuinely concerned about us traveling at night in the icy conditions. Wally, Morning Star, and I discussed it briefly and decided to accept his offer. We set our own campsite along the periphery of the encampment.

We were determined to depart early the next morning, and that we did. Little Wolf reiterated his gratitude and assured us that no harm would come to us from Cheyenne. Moreover, he was determined to share our thoughtfulness with Dull Knife and other Cheyenne encampments.

* * *

The visit with the Cheyenne had been immensely gratifying. We'd listened to God. He'd spoken to our hearts, and we followed His way. Importantly, we kept our scalps. We wished other folks would follow our example but sensed that was not to be. The lure of riches, coupled with a clash of cultures, presented a huge barrier not easily overcome.

We arrived mid-afternoon at the same shelter we'd used on our journey to visit the Cheyenne. While Wally went about building a fire, while Morning Star and I began to collect kindling and logs from around the vicinity to stash away for the benefit of the next visitor to this fine little hideaway.

By the time we'd finished collecting firewood, Wally had the coffee brewing. We would be dining on beef jerky and dried carrots, so washing the feast down with the mountain man's brew was a must. The temperature was dropping, so we seated ourselves on a log before the fire and absorbed its warmth.

I envied Taabe and his pack gnawing away on a fresh kill while I chewed on a strip of tough venison jerky. I swallowed and washed the dry meat down with a swig of coffee. I eyed Wally looking off into the wilderness. "You traveling with us, Wally?" I knew his wanderlust had already kicked in.

He nodded. "Reckon I'll be headin' out in the mornin'," he admitted with his near-toothless grin.

"We appreciate you helping us with the Cheyenne," I

said even though I figured he knew that we were grateful.

"Shucks. Y'all coulda done it yerselves," he drawled. "Yuh sure nuf made some frens."

"There's going to be rough times ahead," I observed. "We're going to need friends."

Wally shook his head resignedly. "Methinks yer right, Isa."

Morning Star thoughtfully poked a stick in the coals. "Wally settle down?" she teased mischievously. She knew the answer, of course.

"Reckon to settle 'bout the time hell freezes o'er," he opined with a laugh. Suddenly, he grew serious. "Had me a love once. Twas way back. Injuns got her." That was Wally's love story in three short sentences.

Morning Star kissed him on the cheek. "We love you, Wally."

"Methinks I'll be turnin' in," he said while wiping away a hint of a tear.

Come morning, Wally was gone. He left us a small sack filled with coffee.

"I wonder whether he'll ever find what he's seeking?" I asked pretty much rhetorically.

Morning Star looked up into my eyes. "Awentia think he has."

I gave her a questioning look.

"Wally keep helping us. He help people. Not so alone as we think."

Morning Star's observation was incredibly profound. She was likely right.

* * *

It was wonderful to return to our ranch. We still basked in the joy of having helped the Cheyenne despite—or more likely because of—their having attacked us.

All was as we had left it. There were no uninvited critters to deal with. Our livestock had learned the value of the baffle, so they headed to it at the first sign of the storm and thus endured the blizzard.

Chapter 13

New Life

We were down to sixteen beeves from the twenty-five my pa had given us as a wedding gift. The weather was warming enough that I worked up a sweat cleaning up the leavings from the livestock after what I hoped was the final snowfall of the winter.

Entering the house, I strode straight to the wash-basin. "Beautiful day," I said as an aside to Morning Star.

She looked up from stirring a pot of stew and blew me a kiss. She turned back to the stove and flinched. Her hand paused over the pot, and the spoon hovered over the stew. She looked at me with widening eyes. A puddle of water began to form at her feet. She dropped the spoon in the pot and took a step back. "Baby come," she announced.

I expect the expression that crossed my face was one of helplessness. Running Waters had told us what to do, but for me, those lessons had gone in one ear and out the other. I wished George's wife was with us at this moment.

"Bed," said Morning Star. "Hot water. Cloths." Her

tone was calm, though I felt she was holding back panic at having to rely on me. She resigned herself to a warrior woman's role in giving birth.

Everything seemed a blur. I stoked the fire and put a pot of water on the stove. I had the good sense to move the stew from the heat. Taabe scratched at the door, and I let him in. It was as though he was curious as to what had broken the morning routine. He looked at Morning Star and back at me before settling back to watch with his head cocked with curiosity and chin on his paws.

"Isa!" called out Morning Star. She had what I understood to be some sort of contraction. Apparently, it had to do with pushing the baby out.

I rushed over to her side.

"Hold hand," she directed me.

I felt as though I needed two more sets of hands.

"Towels," she instructed me.

I released her hand and brought towels and hot water to the bedside.

"Hold hand," she repeated as she strained with another contraction. "Baby come!" she announced through a grimace.

I thought for sure she was going to crush my hand.

"Wet hot cloth," she urged.

This all went on for what seemed like an eternity. And then...a little boy wrapped in a warm towel was snuggling at Morning Star's chest.

My exhausted wife looked up at me through joyful eyes and loving smile. "Need name," she proposed.

It occurred to me that we'd never discussed names. Our son would be of mixed blood, but I felt as though a White man's name would be best and a strong name at that. As part Indian, he'd have to face challenges as he grew to manhood.

Morning Star looked at me expectantly. Names like my lost brother Peter and our friend George floated through my feeble brain. I decided that it should be a biblical name. There were many possibilities. "Moses? Jacob? Joshua? Isaac? Adam?" I didn't realize that I was whispering them aloud.

"Awentia like Moses," came a tired but loving voice from the blankets.

I sat beside her and lifted our child in both hands. "Moses O'Toole, welcome to our home," I said.

"I love you, Isa," cooed Morning Star, as I placed our son beside her. She smiled. "Me tired but hungry."

I went back to the stove to warm up the stew. When I returned with a bowl of the concoction, Morning Star was asleep.

By now, Taabe had grown weary of the show, so I let him out before setting down to enjoy the stew and think on my new role as father.

I stood by the bedside and gazed down lovingly at Moses, nestled asleep in his mother's arms.

* * *

With spring came snowmelt and rains that swelled the Laramie and North Platte rivers. The grasslands turned to a lush green, and buds popped on the cottonwoods, aspens, and oaks. I had a barn and corral to build and had to see to selling our beeves to purchase breeding horses. Quarter Horses were in demand, and I needed to build and train a herd.

George loaned us Hap and Dred to help with construction. The barn was more stable than barn, as it included several stalls for horses. While most would enjoy roaming free on our pasture, the barn and corral would be important for breeding.

Little Moses was a joy, and Morning Star was ever the loving, doting mother to our son.

Spotted Elk came to visit his grandson. He warned us that the rumors of a great gathering of tribes were coming true. We shrugged it off as the fanciful musings of an old warrior. Nevertheless, the warning stuck in the back of my mind.

George and Running Waters came to visit several times, but the most recent one had gotten serious. We were seated around our dining table, enjoying apple pie that Morning Star had baked.

"Lakota chiefs, Crazy Horse, Sitting Bull, and Gall, are moving their camp north to the Greasy Grass," opined George. The Greasy Grass was known to Whites as the Little Bighorn. "Chiefs Lame White Man and Two Moons of the Northern Cheyenne have joined them."

"Do you think there'll be trouble?" I asked.

George nodded.

"Many treaties broken," said Morning Star solemnly, as she nursed Moses.

"The Greasy Grass is a long way north from here," I observed.

"The 7th Cavalry is preparing to head out from Fort Abraham Lincoln. I think they're figuring that Custer can handle the problem," opined George.

"Will be sad day if fight," suggested Morning Star.

"It's worse," lamented George.

I gave him a curious look.

"Some sergeant named Rawlings has convinced Custer that you should scout for them."

My jaw dropped.

Morning Star shook her head. "No," she said firmly.

"We have ranch to build. Lakota, Cheyenne, and Arapaho no bother us." She was right, of course.

The situation having been brought into the open, the patriotic American side of me struggled with Morning Star's logic. The odds against Colonel Custer winning against a huge force of Indians also concerned me. Folks in the know at Fort Laramie said that Custer had barely fought Crazy Horse to a draw when they did battle on the Yellowstone Expedition. Given adequate numbers, the tribes would likely put a whipping on Custer. "They can ask," I said with a knowing smile.

Morning Star, her mind eased for now, sat back and fed Moses.

"They're going to put a lot of pressure on you, Isa. I just reckoned you ought to know." George stood and gazed out the window.

"They can try. I sure don't figure to leave my family." I took a long sip of coffee. I liked Sergeant Rawlings from the Yellowstone adventure and would hate to disappoint him. I thought it was rather ironic that the tribes were gathering at the Little Bighorn to protect their lands from what they saw as an invasion of Whites. It was ironic, because the Lakota had taken those lands from the Crow.

"Chief Gall war chief of Hunkpapa Lakota. Great danger," warned Morning Star.

"The barn and corral are nearly finished. I'm meeting a horse trader next week and have a buyer for ten head of cattle," I said in an attempt to shift the conversation.

Chapter 14

Horses! Horses! Horses!

I reckoned to cross breed eastern Quarter Horses with mustangs. I'd heard that such cross-breeds had an innate cow sense. It was as though they had a natural instinct for working beeves. I knew from accompanying my pa to Bandera, Texas, that the big Texas ranches treasured these western Quarter Horses.

On the appointed day, I bid Morning Star farewell and headed out toward the Circled Cross Ranch. I'd sold the ten beeves, so I had a wad of cash with which to pay the horse trader with whom I'd deal.

George, bless his ever-generous heart, loaned me Hap to help with my negotiations with the horse trader. Hap had a great sense for horseflesh. I'd learned quite a bit from my pa, but I was far from an expert…yet.

"Thanks for joining me, Hap," I said by way of starting a conversation. "I'll be relying on your expertise."

Hap chuckled. "Shucks, Isa. I jus' know poor horse-flesh when I sees it. George don't wanna see yuh be hornswoggled."

"I hear tell that this trader is pretty sharp," I noted.

"Could be sharp at cheatin'," retorted Hap.

"That's where you come in," I advised with a knowing smile.

We were to meet the horse trader at the Immigrants Wash Tub, so we didn't have too long a ride ahead. A wagon train hadn't been seen on the trail for a couple of days, so we figured that the place might be empty of travelers washing clothes and otherwise preparing to tackle the arduous trail ahead. Taabe and his pack followed us at a distance.

Upon arriving at Immigrants Wash Tub, our expectations were met. There was no evidence of any wagon train having recently stopped. It thus wasn't difficult to spot the horse trader. He'd used rope to cordon off a remuda of what appeared at first glance to be a half dozen fine-looking horses.

The trader appeared pretty much as what I expected a livestock speculator to look like here in Wyoming. I'd seen enough cattle speculators when I'd accompanied my pa to Bandera, so this man was no surprise. He was as well-dressed as he appeared to be well-traveled. The man stood a tad under six feet tall, so far as I could tell, and had a lean build. His hat was a tad weatherbeaten, but he wore nice store-bought clothes and black knee-high boots. They bore a light coating of trail dust; no surprise after herding cayuses across the countryside. He seemed to be the real deal. He carried a Colt Peacemaker holstered on his right hip.

We rode over to the man. "Howdy," I greeted. "Are you Mr. Artemus Jackson?"

The trader gave me a squinty-eyed look. "I am," he replied with a glance from me to Hap and back.

Hap and I slipped from our saddles. I extended my hand. "I'm Isa O'Toole, and this is my hand, Hap Cole."

"You bring money?" asked the trader, directing his question at Hap. He was clearly put off by dealing with a half-breed. Nevertheless, the man was wasting no time getting to the point of our meeting.

"Ask the boss," directed Hap with a nod toward me.

"Let's take a look at the horses first," I replied. Something wasn't feeling right about this fellow.

"They're fine stock. Best available," replied the trader. He looked to be uncomfortable recognizing me as the buyer. His prejudice was showing through loud and clear.

I figured that the man's personal views wouldn't matter when it came to dealing in good old US dollars. I smiled, and we began to amble on over to the horses. "You have bills of sale for these broncs?" asked Hap.

"Er…we don't need paperwork," he responded.

My intuition was telling me that something was seriously amiss, and I could see from Hap's body language that he was becoming concerned, too. "Where is this stock from?" I asked.

"Back east," claimed the horse trader.

"Where?" I repeated.

"This is good horseflesh. You're asking too many questions." This man was getting testy.

I looked knowingly at Hap, then kneeled to examine the forelocks of the first horse. As I came up, I reached back and came up with my Bowie knife under the man's nose. I must admit that I was getting right-practiced at placing the tip of the blade under an adversary's nose. "Where is Artemus Jackson?" I demanded.

The man's eyes bulged with fear. If he'd counted on

dealing with a naïve tenderfoot, he'd been soundly mistaken. His right hand hovered over the butt of the revolver in his holster.

"You move that hand closer to your gun, and you'll be breathing through your mouth for the rest of your life," I threatened. "Now, where is Artemus Jackson?"

"I don't know," responded the man.

"Relieve him of that peashooter, Hap."

Hap slipped around behind the man and drew the man's revolver from its holster.

The man had begun to sweat bullets despite the chill air. He was nearly cross-eyed, staring down at the tip of my blade.

With a slight flick of my knife, I nicked his nose.

He pulled back with a start and lifted his hand to his bloodied snout.

"Where's Jackson?" I persisted. "And who are you?" I moved the knife close enough to force him to his knees.

"D-d-don't be cutting me again," he pleaded. "I didn't kill him. He already be dead."

"Dead?" I asked.

"Came upon him, as he lay dying," insisted the man. "Couple of them Indian arrows in his chest. Still had his scalp and the horses, so something scared them off."

"Where is he?"

"Over yonder," he said, pointing beyond the horses. "And my name is Willy Macon."

"Get up, and lead us to him," I directed. Whatever had happened to Jackson must not have happened very long before our arrival.

We soon found ourselves standing over Jackson's body. Sure enough, a pair of Lakota arrows stuck from his chest. His carbine lay beside him. I checked it and found it empty. Apparently, he'd managed to defend himself enough to chase off his attackers. The hostiles must have thought he was still alive when they departed, or they'd have taken his scalp and the horses just as Macon suggested. I scanned the area. There was a great deal of blood on a rock close by. If it belonged to a Lakota warrior, the attackers had taken the body with them.

"How come you didn't bury him?" asked Hap.

"I heard y'all coming up the trail. I didn't even have time to check for bills of sale."

"So, you were going to sell Jackson's horses and take the money from the sale," I stated bluntly.

Macon sighed. "Guilty, I'm afraid."

I wasn't sure what to do with this man. In a sense, he was a horse thief and could be hanged. "What do you think, Hap? We turn this fellow over to the command at Fort Laramie?"

Macon looked at me with imploring eyes.

"Dang, but it's two days to the fort, Isa," observed Hap.

I laid a devious smile on Macon. "We could just hang him and get it over with."

"Y-y-you wouldn't," pleaded Macon.

"You have a horse somewhere?" I asked.

"Back up the trail a piece," responded Macon with a touch of hope in his voice. "I come on this situation after Jackson had been attacked. Had to be mighty careful in case them Indians were hanging around."

While Hap kept an eye on Macon, I found the bills of sale in Jackson's vest pocket.

"Tell you what, Macon. You take that little shovel at yonder laundry sluice and dig a nice grave for Mr.

Jackson here. We'll see to getting his personal effects to Fort Laramie and money to any next of kin."

Macon gazed up at me with an inquisitive expression.

"It's against my better judgment, but we'll set you free. Just don't dare let us catch you in these parts ever again. Is that clear?" I was feeling pretty good about how I was handling this situation. Hap even nodded his approval, though I suspect he'd just as soon have hung the man as a horse thief.

"Thanks. Thanks kindly," said a relieved Willy Macon. "Y'all will never see me near here again." He fetched the shovel and began digging in the rocky soil. We wrapped Jackson in his own blanket and buried him. We fashioned a wood cross and planted it at the head of the grave. Hap carved the man's name and the date into it.

* * *

We now had six eastern Quarter Horses plus the mount Jackson had ridden. The papers showed the cayuses to be legitimate eastern-bred. We stuffed all of the man's personal effects in a saddlebag with a fair amount of money for the horses. There was a photograph in Jackson's bag that depicted a younger version of him, a handsome woman, and two young boys. We reckoned that meant he had some family.

First thing upon arriving at my place, we parked the Quarter Horses in the new corral. I went into the house to share what had happened with Morning Star.

She was rightly proud of how we'd handled the situation up at Emigrant's Wash Tub. After hugs and kisses, she insisted on seeing our investment and came outside to take a gander at the fine horseflesh we had acquired.

"Horses beautiful," she said as she entered the corral. The horses took to her right away, and she was soon stroking necks and muzzles as the cayuses competed for affection. She truly had a way with them. Finally, Morning Star turned to Hap and me. *"Ana o'a hi'it,"* she invited in Comanche. "Come eat," she said for Hap's sake.

"Yes, come grab some grub before you head back to the Circled Cross, Hap." We had decided that there was no point in both of us going to Fort Laramie with Jackson's personal effects, so Hap would stop to tell the story to George and then go on to the fort.

We gathered around the kitchen table, savoring coffee and Morning Star's latest culinary creation. She sure had a way with food, and if I wasn't careful, she'd turn me into a fat old rancher. "Guess you heard about Custer going off to tackle Crazy Horse and Sitting Bull," I ventured.

Hap chuckled. "Yep. George was sayin' they wanna recruit yuh."

"Fat chance," I stated firmly.

Morning Star poured more coffee. "Isa no fight our people."

Hap nodded that he understood where we were coming from. "It ain't an easy choice. Injuns do fight each other as much as Whites," he observed. "But I kin hardly blame y'all."

"If what we hear is true, the Lakota and Cheyenne are fixing for a big battle," I noted. "They may win a couple of fights early on, but the soldiers have better weapons and more men to replace those lost in battle. When Indians lose a warrior, it takes many years to raise and train a replacement. The Northern Cheyenne, Arapaho, and Lakota will meet the same end as the once mighty

Comanche. It is better if they come together in peace and learn White man's ways."

Morning Star stared thoughtfully at me. Finally, she sighed resignedly. "Is sad but true," she lamented.

"Well, as I unnerstan' it, Custer has already departed. Brigadier General George Crook eked out a costly win at what they be callin' the Battle of Rosebud Creek up near the Little Bighorn River. That was just a couple days ago, the 17th of June, I think. Many kilt on both sides. Injuns left the field, so Crook claimed the win."

"Sound like big battle come," offered Morning Star, as she began to nurse Moses much to Hap's discomfort. "Is too late for Isa to join Custer," she said with a relieved smile.

"So, you think a big fight is coming?" I asked Hap.

"Feel it in my bones, Isa." Hap took a long swig of coffee, then stood. "I better head to Circled Cross. Thanks kindly fer the hospitality."

"It's been great to spend time with you, Hap. *Vaya con Dios*." I escorted Hap outside to his cayuse and saw him off. Before heading back inside, I took a long gander at our spread. The Quarter Horses were prancing around the corral, and the afternoon sunlight ricocheted off their muscular bodies. God willing, I was going to reap the bounty of one of His more beautiful creations. We'd be setting to work breeding these horses with wild mustangs to create the line of Quarter Horses that cowboys were craving.

I'd written off to my pa as to what I was planning. He sent a letter to Morning Star and me advising that he was going to send a horse breeder friend to come teach me the finer points of breeding. Any experienced help would be appreciated. While we were pretty much self-sufficient, we weren't rolling in money. We had to get this breeding business underway and then head to Texas to start the other part of our venture.

While I was contemplating the future, I was blithely unaware that Custer was fixing to rendezvous with Brigadier General Terry and Colonel Gibbon and move toward the Bighorn and Little Bighorn Rivers.

* * *

At the very end of June, I headed to George's ranch to meet the breeder that my pa had sent to help me and escort him to my ranch. I'd arisen well before sunup with hopes of enjoying one of Running Waters' fine breakfasts. Morning Star decided to stay home with Moses rather than bring him along in the cradleboard.

As I reined in before George's home, I was struck by a somber feeling.

George strode out onto the gallery to greet me. "Welcome, Isa," he called out.

"Morning. Is Mr. Wilkins here?"

"Yes. He's napping down at the bunkhouse. Moseyed in day before yesterday and was tuckered out. But come inside first and have some coffee."

I hitched Paint and followed George inside. "What's going on?" I queried.

"You haven't heard?"

"Heard what?" I pressed.

"Sad day for Custer. He and better than two hundred fifty of his 7th Cavalry were massacred at Greasy Grass by Indians led by Crazy Horse and Gall. It's already being called Custer's Last Stand." George poured two cups of coffee and handed one to me.

I sat there stunned for a moment. "I heard there was likely to be a big battle, but..."

"I hear that some major named Reno is accusing Custer of miscommunicating, likely to cover his own mistakes. Well, General Sherman won't be standing for it," advised George. "I expect this is the beginning of the end for the Indians. Sherman will throw all he has against them. They haven't the chance of a snowball in hell."

"Glad I wasn't up there scouting for Custer," I responded. "Sad that so much blood was shed. This was sure to happen after gold was discovered in the Black Hills. Miners from everywhere swarmed the place and broke what little was left of any treaties."

"We're fortunate to be a long ride from the Little Bighorn, Isa. That being said, we need to be careful. Once Sherman begins to have his way over the Injuns, it could get dangerous around these parts."

I sighed. "Well, we're fixing to raise horses, George. The more the better. If fighting gets down to our stretch of Wyoming, we'll deal with it." I gazed up at the ceiling, then back to George. "I don't think the tribes will be slowing down the wagon trains hardly at all."

"Sad but likely true, Isa," admitted George.

"Now, this coffee is mighty fine, but let's roust that breeder fellow my pa sent up here."

With that, we walked to the bunkhouse where this Wilkins fellow was still napping. Along the way, George told me I might find the man interesting. Coming from my Black friend, that grabbed my attention. Just what was *interesting* to George?

* * *

Upon entering the bunkhouse, Hap and Dred were sitting in a corner playing cards. They smiled, when they saw me enter and nodded toward the sleeping figure on my old bed.

I shrugged and strolled over to the man. Despite the noise of our entry, Wilkins was snoring like a locomotive. "Mr. Wilkins!" I called out. "Burt Wilkins!" I said louder.

Wilkins snorted, rolled his eyes, and went back to snoring.

I began to understand what George meant by interesting. Wilkins was older than I'd expected. He had white hair tied back behind his head. Under his oversized nose was a huge silver mustache. His face was about as wrinkled as a prune, and half an ear was missing. As he lay on the bed, I reckoned that he couldn't be much over five feet tall. What had my pa sent to me? I bent over closer to his ear. "Wilkins!" I shouted.

The man sat bolt upright, eyes opened wide. "That's me!" he exclaimed.

"Mr. Wilkins, I'm Isa O'Toole," I said with my hand extended.

He brought his eyes into focus on me. "Oh, yer the fella I be seekin'. Yer pa done sent me." He looked down at my hand but ignored it.

George walked up behind me. "Are you up for some dinner, Mr. Wilkins?"

I shook my head and gazed at George. "Interesting," I said.

Off we went to dine with George and his family.

Wilkins was right quiet as he took a seat across from me and stared at the heap of culinary delights that Running Waters and Esmeralda had prepared. I glanced up and caught Wilkins with bowed head, one eye open, and looking around as George gave the blessing. "Amen," he said emphatically as George concluded.

"Where you hail from, Mr. Wilkins?" I asked with my mouth full of egg.

"Don't be talkin' with yer mouth full," ordered Wilkins. "Young'uns these days got no manners," he mumbled.

I swallowed hard.

"I hail from Bandera, son. An' yuh kin call me Burt." He gave a broad, mostly toothless smile. "Yer pa says you be itchin' to raise hosses."

I took a sip of coffee and nodded. I swallowed a bite of sausage. "Got my breeding stock of Quarter Horses just a week ago. Reckon to mate them with mustangs."

"Yuh be makin' fine cowboy stock," observed Wilkins.

"I can hardly wait to get one," said George.

Wilkins smiled. "Might take a year or two," he noted. "Gotta flush out any bad stock." As he finished his sentence, he caught my face flushing with disappointment. "Gotta do it right, Isa. Good stock will keep them cowpokes comin' back regler-like."

"Guess we'll make do," I said. Money would be a tad lean while we waited to breed enough fine stock to sell. It occurred to me that Wilkins might be expecting payment. "Er…what are we going to owe you for your help?"

"Yer pa got me outta a jam. I owe him. Jus' feed me an' keep the rain off my head fer a couple of months," he said with an earnest smile. "I be settin' yuh straight on breedin' them fine critters."

We made small talk while finishing breakfast, then strolled out to the corral. While Wilkins gathered his outfit, I watched a particularly handsome chestnut stallion prance about.

"Yuh like him?" Wilkins startled me, as he

approached the corral with his tack. He gave a low whistle, and the stallion rushed over to him.

"Yours?"

"Sorta," responded Wilkins. "He's his own hoss. Happens tuh tolerate me."

We were soon mounted up and saying our farewells to the George and Running Waters. I reckoned we'd get to my house by mid-afternoon.

Chapter 15

Breeding Quarter Horses

As short-statured and aged as Wilkins was, I was amazed at how well he sat a horse. It seemed as though he and the horse were one.

Wilkins scanned the countryside as we rode toward my humble ranch. "Mighty fine scenery y'all got in these parts," he observed.

"Thanks kindly, Burt. It's sure different from Texas. Winters here are rough."

Wilkins threw another toothless smile at me. "I trapped beaver way north of here long afore I got to Texas. Fought them Blackfoot Lakota savages. Nearly cost me my hair." His eyes sparked a bit at the memory. "Them was the days."

"How'd you wind up in Texas?" Wilkins had gotten my curiosity up.

"Injuns stole my plews an' mules. Them beasts was ornery anyhow." He chuckled to himself. "I headed east an' met a wagon trail on thet thar Oregon Trail. He told me he missed raisin' beeves in Texas. Then and there, I decided to be a cowboy."

"And?" I pressed.

"I signed on to an outfit an' fell in love with hosses. They done captured my heart. Not so ornry as mules. Sweat beasts."

"You bred horses?" I asked.

He gave me an *of course* expression. "Seemed like I could talk to hosses with this here brain." He pointed to his head. "Yer pa told me a bit 'bout yuh, Isa? Yuh like it here?"

I nodded, then paused. I could have sworn that I'd heard a distant rifle shot coming from the general direction of my home, but I couldn't be certain. I shrugged it off.

I went on to share my story of the vision quest, dealing with Crazy Horse, and my life with Morning Star. Before we knew it, we were nearly at my home. As we drew near, I was struck by a queasy feeling. I sensed that something unexpected had happened. There was no immediate sign of any conflict, so there hadn't been an Indian attack.

I dismounted and led Paint the last few yards to the house. Wilkins dropped from his saddle and followed me. I heard a whimpering from one side of the house. I dropped Paint's reins and slipped the Spencer carbine from its scabbard. "Stay here, Burt," I whispered. "I'll call you, if I need you."

I tiptoed to the front corner of the house and peered around at where the sound was coming from. My eyes went wide in amazement. There stood Morning Star with her Henry carbine pointed at a huge furry lump on the ground. Taabe was gnawing away at it along with a couple wolves from his pack. Mua stood beside him with bleeding slashes across her shoulder.

Sensing my arrival, Morning Star looked up at me.

"Bear!" That single word told the story. The grizzly had been nosing around and ran afoul of Taabe and the pack. The bear had taken a swipe at Mua, as she sought to protect her young from the threat. Morning Star heard the commotion, ran outside with her carbine, and encountered the grizzly standing upright and threatening the wolves. She yelled to distract him. He had apparently turned to face her. One snarl and she put a bullet up the boar's snout and between his eyes. He likely tried a paw swipe or two before he dropped dead.

"Thank God you are safe," I said.

"Taabe strong *sunipu*," she assured me.

"I think Awentia strong *sunipu*," I responded. I walked over and lifted the dead bear's head. It was broad and heavy. I stood and hugged Morning Star. "God is good."

Wilkins walked up behind me. "What's this God business?" he called out.

I looked nonchalantly over my shoulder at him, as though killing a bear was an everyday occurrence. "Awentia, this here is Burt Wilkins. He's going to help us breed the horses."

Morning Star caught my game. "Pleased to meet you, Mr. Wilkins. You like bear for dinner?" She asked with a laugh.

"I meant to tell you that I call her my warrior wife," I joked at Wilkins.

"Thet's fine shootin', ma'am," said Wilkins with a heartfelt earnestness.

"Bear looking to attack horses," noted Morning Star. "Taabe save them."

Wilkins suddenly realized that the wolves were not only there but were part of my family. "Yer pa said yer name meant wolf in Comanch language. These frens of y'all."

I nodded and gave Morning Star another hug. "I'm proud of you. You nailed that bear solid." I was truly impressed by her achievement. I reached down and hefted Mua in my arms. "Let's get Mua patched up."

Turning to Wilkins, I said, "We'll check the horses after we care for Mua."

What could he say? He looked as though I'd opened a new world to him. I sensed that his mind was harkening back to his days trapping the beaver among the wildlife of the mountains and rivers. He'd found himself with a pair of teenagers befriended by wolves and dealing with a marauding bear like a normal happening. His musing was broken by a baby's cry. He glanced from me to Morning Star and back to me. "Y'all got a li'l one?"

"Moses hungry," said Morning Star.

I lifted Mua and led the way into the house with a fully amazed Wilkins following us.

"God sure nuf bin right good to y'all," Wilkins observed with a heartfelt tone to his voice. "Hope them Injuns don't be takin' it from yuh. They loves hosses."

Wilkins had hit the proverbial nail on its head. Horses were valuable in general and especially so to Indians. Warrior wealth was measured in large part by the number of horses he owned. Often, the success of a raid was measured in the number of horses that had been captured. "We get along well with the nearby Lakota and Cheyenne...Crow, too. Arapaho pretty much stay south of here, though I hear that they were with Crazy Horse at Little Bighorn."

"Yuh heard 'bout Little Bighorn did yuh?" asked Wilkins.

"I expect that most folks have by now," I replied. "Morning Star and I think it's the beginning of the end for the Indians. Sitting Bull has high-tailed it, taking his Hunkpapa Lakota north to Canada."

While Wilkins and I sipped coffee, Morning Star applied a poultice and bandage to Mua. Taabe's mate looked as though she'd be alright. She looked up from her handiwork and smiled at me. "You get bear skin?"

I'd nearly forgotten. I hoped that Taabe hadn't ripped the dead grizzly's hide too much by now. "Burt. Grab yonder skinning knife and come along," I urged.

Wilkins gazed at me as though wondering whether we'd ever look over my Quarter Horse breeding stock. Nevertheless, he dutifully grabbed the knife from the table beside the door and followed me to the grizzly carcass.

Taabe backed off from the dead bear and moved his pack a short distance away. Wilkins and I went to work skinning the bear, tossing the meat and bone to the wolf pack as we proceeded.

"I nearly fergot this part of frontier life," observed Wilkins. "Woulda thought nuthin' of this thuty yeahs back." He was totally enjoying himself.

"Pleased to have your help," I said.

Soon, we were the proud possessors of a bear skin, and the bellies of Taabe and his pack were full. It remained to tan the hide and decide whether it would make a good rug or even a winter coat. It wasn't long before Mua limped out to rejoin the pack. She looked tired but should heal up good as new.

Wilkins was more than ready to begin my education in breeding Quarter Horses.

* * *

Wilkins had spent a good two hours examining each of the half dozen Quarter Horses that I'd purchased. He did everything but crawl inside each horse. He shunted the three mares into the second section of the corral, likely something I should have thought of.

"Well, come set a spell, Isa," he finally said, patting the top rail of the corral.

I dutifully hopped up on the rail.

Morning Star came out to join us with Moses in the cradleboard. She'd seen Lakota ponies bred, but this would be something new that she needed to know about.

"Yuh done lucked out, son. These hosses got great what folks call conformation. They have fine attitude, too." He chuckled. "Note that I separated the grooms from the brides. At least one of yer grooms got frisky, so yonder chestnut mare is preggers."

I gulped.

"Not to worry. It happens." He waved his hand at the stallions. "We don't have no histry of these fine hosses, so we be makin' it from here on. These three are what yuh call studs. The mares are breeders." He glanced over to be sure I was paying attention. "Yuh got any mustangs yet?"

"About a dozen are grazing just south of here. Take but a couple of hours to gather them."

"That quick?" asked Wilkins with raised eyebrows.

I smiled. "They're all saddle broke. No wild cayuses in the herd, so they're easy to round up."

"Expect that'll keep out any wild streaks in the breed," observed Wilkins.

Morning Star laughed. "They saddle broke, but much spirit."

"That's good to know," noted Wilkins. "A Quarter Hoss with spirit...that be good." He looked over at the barn. "Y'all got all the fixins. Plenty room in yer barn, lots of pasture, water close by, good feed, and stalls set off fer breedin'."

Morning Star and I were pleased that Wilkins approved of our layout.

"Y'all got a calendar?" he asked.

I responded with a blank look.

"Yer gonna have to keep track of the breedin' cycles of yer mares. It be important to know when them brides be ready fer the groom." He chuckled at his own humor. "Once them mares be in heat, they gotta git to know their stallions. They need to get along. Yuh got a couple of strong studs there. Yuh might have to hold them back just a tad."

This was getting interesting. I had reckoned to clumsily put the Quarter Horses and mustangs together and let nature take its course.

"When yuh sell yer stock to the cowpokes, they gotta know the breedin' be solid," advised Wilkins. "Lemme go on. Once yer mares be preggers, it be somethin' like eleven months afore they foal."

We did know how long the pregnancy lasted, so this was no surprise.

"Once they be ready to foal, yuh just need to give 'em a clean, quiet stall with plenty of space. Best if y'all are with the mare in case there be any problem." Wilkins laughed. "Once yuh got a foal, it needs momma's milk right soon. Momma will help the little thang stand."

"Thanks, Burt. There's plenty we didn't know."

Wilkins smiled at being appreciated. "Once y'all got them colts runnin' aroun', the bizness of selling them to cowpokes begins. Expect yer pa might help with that. Couple years an' y'all will have a reputation. Pokes be lookin' fer yer brand."

"Brand?" I exclaimed. "We never…"

"Y'all should name yer ranch an' register a brand. Pokes wanna know where to come."

Morning Star and I looked at each other. We'd toyed with naming our spread but hadn't come up with anything. Pa ran the Rising Cross Ranch, and George had his Circled Cross Ranch. There were big outfits like the King Ranch, named for its owner, and the JA Ranch down on the Texas Panhandle. "We need to think on this, Burt."

"Take yer sweet time. Gonna be ten months or so afore yonder mare foals," he said with a smile. "Yer others, a tad longer. We gotta get yer studs meetin' with them mustang mares."

"I can round them up in the morning, Burt."

* * *

We began the process of acquainting our studs with the mustang mares. These foals would be bred for speed and agility. Once we had accomplished this process, we reckoned to introduce mustang stallions to the two remaining Quarter Horse mares. We figured they would produce strong conformation and the best traits of both breeds. Time would tell. Once we'd done our part and the horses had mated, the outcome would be in God's hands.

Wilkins hung around for another month. He assured us that he foresaw no complications.

Well, we named our ranch the Laramie Cross Breed Ranch. It combined our location with what we did while doubling as a reference to our faith. The brand was a cross atop a mountain peak.

The toughest part of breeding was selecting the best

matches. Once a stallion had done his duty, he was let to pasture. We duly recorded all of the matings. We were determined that cowboys would value the fine Quarter Horses we bred, and that word would spread. Soon, all the mares were pregnant, and the stallions romped freely in the surrounding pasture, finding their way to the corral at dusk. What could possibly go wrong?

Chapter 16

Unwanted Visit

I was mucking stalls when I heard it. The telltale jingling and rattling of sabers, creaking of saddle leather, and clip-clopping hooves on rocky turf announced the approach of six cavalry troopers led by some wet-behind-the-ears lieutenant.

I strolled uneasily from the barn, while Morning Star emerged from our front door with Moses on her hip. Her hair was in a long braid, and she wore her buckskins this day.

The lieutenant led his men up to the front of our house. They had the guidon of Company K of the 2nd US Cavalry. "Good morning. I'm Lieutenant Dickerson. Is the master home? I'm looking for an Isa O'Toole."

Hearing the officer's prejudice-laced greeting immediately put me on edge. "That's my wife you're addressing, Lieutenant," I stated firmly, as I strode toward the patrol.

Dickerson gave me a once-over. "You O'Toole?"

"That's Mr. O'Toole to you," I responded.

"Didn't know you were a breed," he observed with a

half-sneer. He had a long nose appropriate to be looking down at folks he deemed beneath his station in life.

I controlled my displeasure, as surely God would have me do. About this time, Taabe and his pack appeared from the side of our house.

Upon seeing the wolves, the lieutenant pulled back hard on his reins and began to draw his revolver.

Morning Star quickly snatched the shotgun that had been hidden just behind the doorjamb and pointed the muzzle at the officer.

"You yank that gun any further, Lieutenant, and my wife will blow your head off."

The troopers were sitting their saddles with horrified looks on their faces. Apparently, no one ever got away with confronting their dandified lieutenant. They chattered in a mix what I'd later learn was German with Irish sprinkled in.

"What did you say?" snarled Dickerson.

By now, I had moved beside Morning Star and had my own Spencer in hand. I was struggling to contain my temper. "Those wolves won't harm a hair of your head unless you hurt me. I don't know why you are here, but if you can't be civil, I invite you to leave."

The lieutenant laid a steely gaze into my eyes as though judging how far he might push me. He finally took his hand off the butt of his revolver and reached into his tunic. He drew out a sealed envelope. "I've been ordered to deliver this to Mr. Isa O'Toole," he said and tossed it at me.

I'd had enough. "Guess the cavalry no longer teaches its officers to be men of honor," I declared.

Dickerson flinched a tad. "Sad the Army recruits breeds for scouts," he huffed.

"You ever fight an Indian, Lieutenant?" I challenged.

His expression said no.

"Well, if an Indian captures you, you'll understand why the Army hires men of Indian blood so the sorry likes of you can keep their hair. Now, get off my land." I raised the muzzle of my Spencer for good measure.

Dickerson sat upright. "I'm supposed to wait while you open the envelope…sir."

The begrudged *sir* stuck in my craw. I reckoned that in a fight, I'd put a solid licking on the scrawny bag-of-bones of an officer that Dickerson was. Then again, there was no point in forcing those fine troopers behind him to arrest me. It wasn't their fault that God had planted Dickerson on this earth. "Why don't you put your men at ease, Lieutenant. They're welcome to water their horses at yonder trough." The least I could do was be hospitable to the troopers. I winked at Morning Star and tore open the envelope.

Dickerson permitted his men to dismount and water their horses.

I purposely took my time unfolding and reading the message. Upon first reading, I handed it to Morning Star to read.

Dickerson impatiently sat his steed. He was sweating in his woolen tunic.

Morning Star handed the paper back to me. I paused thoughtfully and reread it. In my peripheral vision, I could see that Dickerson was stewing.

"Sir?" Dickerson pressed.

"General George Crook is requesting—not ordering me, mind you—requesting me to serve as a scout at Fort Laramie." I paused as though seriously considering my response. I had already decided, but enjoyed watching the arrogant, prejudiced officer sweat a bit more. I expect I wasn't exactly being a good Christian, but it felt nearly as good as putting that whipping on the man. He surely needed one. "I've never met General Crook, and I'm sure he's a fine soldier with a job to do after the loss at Little Bighorn." I wanted to call the place Greasy Grass but figured that the lieutenant wouldn't understand. "We have built excellent relations with the tribes here. If I were to join the troops, it would place those relations in danger, as they'd see us as the enemy."

Lieutenant Dickerson stared at me. Deep inside, he knew that what I said made perfect sense. However, he was still every bit the pompous, pretentious, self-serving human and a spit-and-polish officer in George Crook's command. "Would you please sign the message and return it to me. You may use an *X* as necessary."

"Are you familiar with Socrates, Lieutenant?"

Dickerson blushed. "Some Greek?"

"Well, how about that! I'll bet you can even sign your name!" I turned the verbal screws on the officer.

The troopers had overheard and were murmuring and guffawing to themselves at how their lieutenant had been shown up by a teenage Wyoming rancher.

I signed the message and added a note to the effect that I respectfully turned down his request. "I'd be pleased to explain my reason to the general in person, Lieutenant, if you're not up to giving it to him straight." I handed him the message.

Dickerson ordered his men to mount up, gave me a half-baked salute, nodded to Morning Star, and headed off to Fort Laramie.

"Blue coat funny," observed Morning Star, as we watched the troopers fade into the distance.

"I pray he survives out here. He's the kind that is hard to teach. His mind is closed."

Morning Star led me back inside. We sipped coffee

and ate bear sign while Moses nursed. Once he was fed and sleeping, we enjoyed our bearskin rug.

* * *

I suppose General Crook must have given up on me, as we received no further messages, nor visits. We fairly regularly saw prairie schooners wending their way westward on the Oregon Trail, a mile or so off to the north of us. This continued despite the threat of Indian attacks.

With Crook's troopers off chasing hostiles, the garrison at Fort Laramie was reduced somewhat. We occasionally saw patrols but heard of no engagements in the vicinity. Folks anxiously awaited the capture of Crazy Horse, Sitting Bull, and the other chiefs while mining towns sprung up here and there. One new mining town we heard about was up in western Dakota in the Black Hills. It was called Deadwood. I wondered whether it would amount to anything or disappear like so many other towns when the gold played out.

Morning Star and I appreciated that I was here with her and not chasing about through the mountains as a scout for Crook. Aside from risking my life, it would have seriously hampered our horse breeding operations.

Now and then, George would bring Hap and Dred by to see how we were doing. They'd pitch in with a chore or two. Our Black rancher friend updated us on what he'd heard out of Fort Laramie as to Crook's progress with the Indians. We learned that Sitting Bull had led his Hunkpapa Lakota far north into Canada with hopes of waiting out the blue coat onslaught.

Occasionally, we'd ride over to the Circled Cross and dine with the Freemans. We reciprocated, as George had a special hankering for Morning Star's stew.

We had our hands full with ensuring that the needs of all our expectant mares were met. Our greatest challenge arrived with the first blizzard of the winter. We'd had the sense to build a section of the barn for our Quarter Horse stallions. While they were a hearty breed, we were intent on protecting them from the frigid weather as far as possible. The barn afforded warm shelter and plenty of feed. The mustangs, on the other hand, used the baffle to shelter from the winter storms. George had acquired horse blankets from Fort Laramie for us to use. We had enough of these blankets to keep most of our mustangs a tad warmer.

With the snow came more time inside our toasty stone house. We had plenty of firewood and food. I thanked the Lord that I'd seen fit to dig our well within the walls of our home. Fetching water out in raging snowstorms was decidedly undesirable. Following George's example, we laid ropes from our house to the barn, so we wouldn't get lost going from one to the other in a whiteout storm. Meanwhile, we had many months yet ahead of us before our mares would foal.

* * *

I reckon fate often holds a built-in touch of irony. It was a mid-January day. A blizzard had roared through the day before, shrouding the already snow-covered landscape in another considerable layer of ice. I shielded my eyes from the sun and glare, as I moseyed out our front door to go check on the horses gathered around the baffle. I looked off at the Laramie Range, lingering about ten miles off to our west. I never tired of appreciating the rugged beauty of its snowy peaks and valleys. All was silent. There wasn't even a breeze to disrupt the post-storm stillness.

So it was, that I saw an unusual lump in the snow atop a hill a couple of hundred yards to the north of our house. I poked my head back inside and alerted Morning Star. "There's something out yonder that I should check. Might be a horse or elk that was felled by the blizzard."

"Call me if you need help," she responded.

I grabbed my Spencer carbine and headed to the lump. I approached cautiously. Whatever lay there wasn't moving. As I closed in, I realized that it was a horse frozen to death. Enough snow had blown from it to reveal the tack of a cavalry mount. I felt the horse's flank. It was quite dead. The snow had drifted up over the horse's underbelly. As I shrugged and was about to turn back to the house, I heard a weak groan. I pulled back the flap of my bearskin hat and strained my ears in the frigid cold. I heard the groan again.

Rushing to the other side of the horse, I realized that a human was wedged against the underside of the dead beast. Whomever it was, had used the horse for shelter and tried to draw as much heat as possible from it. My gloved hands were soon scraping snow and ice, revealing the woolen tunic of a trooper. He was alive! He was covered in ice but still breathing.

He was nearly frozen to the horse, but I managed to wrench him free and begin the arduous task of dragging him to the house. Fortunately, he wasn't a big man, as I struggled to breathe in the frigid air.

Morning Star's mouth gaped, as I dragged the half-frozen human across our threshold. She ran for blankets, as I began to strip the icy, wet clothing from the trooper.

I finally got a look at his face. It was Lieutenant Dickerson! The man was near death's door. I wondered at how he'd gotten separated from his unit and why they'd been out in the blizzard, but those questions would have to wait. With Morning Star's help, we got him wrapped in blankets in front of our hearth. We rubbed his hands and feet in an attempt to restore circulation. Somehow, the Lord had protected him from frostbite, but it was danged close to it. If I hadn't seen him and gone out to check the lump in the snow, he'd surely have frozen to death.

* * *

I reckon an hour passed. Morning Star and I had done all we could. We sipped coffee while we waited for Dickerson to awaken from his cold-induced slumber. Morning Star had warm soup prepared for when he came to.

"Wh-where am I?" came the barely-audible murmur from an awakening lieutenant.

I stood silently, took a sip of coffee, and strode over to Dickerson. I kneeled beside him. Morning Star went over to fill a bowl with soup. "Lieutenant Dickerson? Can you hear me?"

Dickerson's eyes flitted a bit and then opened. "Where…oh…you."

"Brought you in from out yonder, Lieutenant. You were nearly frozen to death beside your horse."

"The men? What about…?" His weakened voice trailed off.

I raised the officer's head, while Morning Star put a spoonful of soup to his lips.

He swallowed. This was a good sign.

"I didn't see your men, Lieutenant."

Dickerson took another spoonful of soup, and his

eyes opened. "Caught in storm," he lamented. His eyes widened, as he realized who had saved him. "Y-you. You be the Injuns..."

I smiled. "Welcome to the Laramie Cross Breed Ranch, Lieutenant Dickerson. We're pleased to have saved your life."

Tears came to his eyes. He was searching for words to overcome his prejudice. "Thank you."

"Where were y'all when the storm hit?" I probed.

"Twenty-four troopers. Running fight with Arapaho. Lost three men killed, four wounded." Dickerson was plumbing the depths of his thawing-out memory. "Heading back to Fort Laramie, when storm hit."

Blizzards up here could hit quick and hard, catching folks inexperienced with Wyoming winters unaware. "So, you were separated from your company?" I asked the obvious.

Dickerson gave a weak nod. "Seems so." He tried to sit up, but his body wouldn't permit it.

"Just relax, Lieutenant. Rest. When you're fit to stand, we'll get you to Fort Laramie."

The officer swallowed another spoonful of soup from Morning Star before closing his eyes and drifting off to slumber.

Morning Star gently stroked my cheek. "Isa save life. Man owe life debt."

I recalled my pa telling of how his friend, Spirit Talker, had assumed a life debt when Pa saved him from a mountain lion. The debt was repaid many times and reciprocated to the point that it was meaningless. Nevertheless, it had been the catalyst for an enduring friendship. Given Dickerson's deep-seated prejudices, I doubted he'd have any thought of owing me a debt for saving his life. "I don't reckon to ever collect it, sweetheart," I said with a crooked smile.

* * *

While the lieutenant was sleeping, I went back out to where I'd found him and managed to retrieve the tack from his dead horse, as well as his rifle, saber, and saddlebags. I wondered whether his company had made it back to the fort. Time would tell. I prayed that they endured the storm and arrived safely. If so, a search patrol might be sent out to find Lieutenant Dickerson and any stragglers. The winter here in Wyoming could be a brutal master, and it had quite apparently taught the 2nd US Cavalry a hard lesson.

It was around dusk as I was sitting at our kitchen table softening a fox pelt that Dickerson awakened.

The lieutenant managed to sit up and rub more circulation back into his fingers. He took a long, studied look at me. "Guess I'm obliged to you, Mr. O'Toole." His words no longer hung so grudgingly. I'm not sure what thoughts swirled in his head.

"You think you can stand, Lieutenant?" I asked.

He nodded weakly.

Morning Star and I lifted him to a chair. It was a good first step. We slid a small table beside him, and Morning Star filled a bowl with hot stew and delivered it to him along with a biscuit and coffee.

Dickerson gratefully polished off the grub. "Dark?" he asked.

I nodded.

Between the darkness and a precipitous drop in temperature, he resigned himself to spending the night as our guest. "Guess I've been a fool," he said sheepishly.

"I don't deserve this from you folks." He sighed. "I'm sorry."

We didn't react to his admission, though we were touched by it. "We're glad you survived, Lieutenant. We'll see to getting you to Fort Laramie come morning, if you're up to traveling."

I realized that Fort Laramie was two days off, so I reckoned to stop at George's ranch rather than push hard through the frozen terrain. I rather looked forward to it, as I was curious to meet the general whose scouting request I had turned down.

* * *

Lieutenant Dickerson and I rode with care on the icy approach to Fort Laramie. George had decided to join us just in case any hostiles took an interest in us along the way from his ranch. An extra gun never hurts, especially in these uncertain times.

The gate sentry's face lit up with surprise at the sight of Lieutenant Dickerson. It took but moments for a small welcome detail to form.

Dickerson found the energy to sit nearly ramrod-straight in his saddle and salute.

George and I followed along quietly. I did want to meet General Crook. I knew that his command had won the much-debated victory at the Battle of the Rosebud, and the debacle endured by Custer had been under his command.

This was Dickerson's play now. He strove to appear as dignified as possible as he led us to the fort headquarters. He reined in and addressed the corporal standing guard. "Lieutenant Dickerson reporting," he said, returning the guard's salute. "Is the general in?"

"General Crook has been waiting, sir," replied the corporal. "I'll let him know that you've arrived, sir."

Dickerson stole a glance at us and managed a weak smile, as we all waited patiently to be ushered in to see the general.

"General Crook will see you now, sir," said the corporal upon reemerging from the headquarters. He gave a measured look at George and me but said nothing.

Dickerson dismounted and motioned for us to follow him. We followed him into Crook's office.

The lieutenant came to attention and gave a soldierly salute. "Lieutenant Dickerson reporting from patrol, sir."

"At ease, Lieutenant," Crook said while giving us a once-over. "Who have you brought with you, Lieutenant?"

"Sir, this is George Freeman who owns the Circled Cross Ranch, a day's ride west of here on the Oregon Trail. This young gentleman saved my life. His name is Isa O'Toole, and he owns the Laramie Cross Breed Ranch."

Crook immediately caught on to the wordplay in the name of my ranch. "Quarter Horses, I hope?" he said.

"Yes, sir," I responded. "Breeding them with mustangs."

Crook nodded. He apparently understood good horseflesh. He paused in thought while we waited anxiously to hear what was on his mind. Recognition swept across his face. "You're the young fellow that Colonel Stanley recommended as a scout," he stated bluntly.

"I scouted on the Yellowstone Expedition, sir."

"You turned me down, but my offer stands. I will be joining General Terry up near Deadwood in the Dakota

Territory next summer to put a whipping on the Lakota hostiles. I'll soon be heading out and could use good scouts."

"You could use great horses, too, General," I replied. "My wife and I are raising a family just beyond George's ranch, and have a bunch of Quarter Horses and mustangs nearly ready to foal. We are at peace with the local tribes."

"If I may, General, Mr. O'Toole is part Comanche and his wife is a Miniconjou Lakota."

"Go ahead, Lieutenant." Crook waved his hand for Dickerson to continue.

"Mr. O'Toole saved me from nearly freezing to death in the recent blizzard. I was separated from my company in a running battle with Arapaho, and the storm hit before we could regroup. I became lost in the storm, but by God's good graces, I fell close to Mr. O'Toole's home. He and his wife took me in, thawed me out, and helped me return here to Fort Laramie."

Crook nodded approvingly and turned to me. "I'm grateful for your service, Mr. O'Toole. We need more folks in these parts like you and your wife." He looked at Dickerson. "Lieutenant, I assume you came straight here upon your arrival. You will become aware upon return to barracks that all but four of your company made it back to Fort Laramie in the face of the blizzard. Given the circumstances of the storm, I cannot hold you to account for the loss of men or your separation from your unit. Even finding shelter from the storm may not have been the best decision. I'm pleased that you are back with us and can resume your duties. This has surely been an educational experience."

Dickerson came to attention. "Thank you, sir."

Crook stood and extended his hand to me and then

George. His eyes locked on mine. "Again, I deeply appreciate you saving Lieutenant Dickerson's life. If you change your mind and wish to scout for me, I would welcome it. Meanwhile, I'm authorizing you to help yourself to what ammunition and foodstuffs you might need from our quartermaster." The general scribbled a few sentences on an official-looking piece of stationery. "Just hand this to my quartermaster."

"Thank you right kindly, General," I responded.

"If I get back here, I might look you up to snag one of your Quarter Horses." He faced Dickerson. "Lieutenant, you are dismissed." He returned Dickerson's salute, and we exited.

I surely hadn't expected any reward for saving the lieutenant, but I wasn't about to turn down the general's largesse. As we left the headquarters, I addressed Dickerson. "I pray you'll enjoy a long and illustrious career, Lieutenant." I extended my hand, which he gripped solidly.

"Thank you again, Isa O'Toole. I apologize again for my behavior at our first meeting. I wish you and your lovely wife success in your breeding enterprise." Dickerson headed to check on his men, while George and I made a beeline for the quartermaster.

It struck me how an unwanted visit had turned out so well. I glanced up to the crystal blue sky and praised God.

Chapter 17

Foals Galore!

Spring finally arrived, and with it, foaling. It was hard to believe that eleven months had passed. We'd be recording each birth as advised by Wilkins, so we would gradually ensure our very own consistent breed of Quarter Horses. It was essential that cowboys could rely on the stock of the Laramie Cross Breed Ranch.

We'd written down Wilkins' instructions on the birth process and how to handle any complications. Morning Star had seen plenty of ponies born during her early years with her Lakota people, and I had been through the process with both cattle and horses on our ranch in Texas. Each birth seemed like its own miracle, even in the couple that caused us to awaken in the middle of the night.

Before long, we were blessed not with the expected six foals, but seven. One of our mustang mares foaled twins. It was a bit rougher as the birthing went, but we saw her through it just fine.

Our herd of horses had now burgeoned to six pure-bred Quarter Horses and seven cross-breeds, and about a dozen mustangs. Our mustang herd also grew, as the mustang stallions out in our far pasture found a half dozen mares in heat. I reckoned that we'd be ready to begin taking some of our stock to market by the spring of '78. With profits, we'd add additional eastern-bred Quarter Horses. All we had to do was weather another winter and pray that we weren't visited by hostile Indians. We'd also have another round of mating, such that we'd maintain a constant turnover of stock while expanding the herd.

* * *

One of my concerns was saddle-breaking our broncs. I was intent on delivering top-quality Quarter Horses that were ready to ride. Each individual buyer would have to train the cayuse to their own preferences, but at least they wouldn't be bucking around a corral. To that end, Morning Star and I came up with an idea that drew from my pa's having found drovers for his cattle drives by recruiting soldiers leaving the military service. I reckoned we'd start by offering any qualified trooper from Fort Laramie the opportunity to earn a few extra dollars. Our hope was that after we sold some of our horses, we could afford to lure them from the cavalry and hire them full-time. To that end, I began construction of a modest bunkhouse near the barn and corrals.

I reckoned it wouldn't be long before we'd head to Texas and begin the second part of our ranching business. My pa had already offered to give us a piece of Rising Cross Ranch and a few beeves.

By the time our first colts were ready for saddle-breaking, we'd had another foaling and more expectant mares. We diligently kept our mating and foaling records.

Meanwhile, General Crook was conducting his Powder River campaigns against the Lakota and Cheyenne. The tribes were grudgingly losing ground under the steady assault. The US government had a vastly superior array of resources, from manpower to weapons and supplies. The Indians could not replace their fighting men in sufficient numbers and were woefully weak in weaponry. Crazy Horse wound up at the Red Cloud Agency but yearned to return to the traditional life of the Lakota. Jealousies developed between Crazy Horse and fellow Lakota chiefs, Spotted Tail and Red Cloud. Coupled with rumors of Crazy Horse's threat to kill General Crook, the chief wound up being stabbed to death by a Lakota guard at Fort Robinson. It was said that Crazy Horse had a dream in which he was killed by his own people, so this fulfilled that vision.

Our ranching operations went smoothly during 1877 with no trouble from neighboring tribes. It was a time during which we could easily lapse into complacency. We worked constantly at improving ranch operations. Morning Star and I did hunt. At first, Moses would accompany us in his cradleboard. By the time he was big enough to take his first steps, I had fashioned a rig by which he could ride behind one of us. He loved it. Importantly, it acquainted him with the frontier. Thus, we successfully hunted pronghorn, elk, deer, bobcat, bear, and more.

We didn't live by meat alone. We planted a large section of pasture to raise feed grain and vegetables for our consumption. It brought back memories of how my nomadic Comanche ancestors were forced to establish a reading network to balance their diet, which was heavy with buffalo.

* * *

By 1878, we were ready to begin saddle-breaking our horses. A private named Jim Hale was the first to take us up on our offer to saddle-break horses, though he didn't last long. Hale had grown up on a ranch in Texas and garnered some experience before he'd joined the 2nd Cavalry. Unfortunately, he took an arrow in his leg on one of Crook's Powder River expeditions and was lost for the season to the rigors of busting broncs.

So it was that Corporal Chester Donovan showed up one morning. I responded to a knock at our front door.

I took a gander through the peephole, then swung the big door open. I found myself looking at an average-sized but muscular young man wearing cavalry trousers and boots, but with a red plaid shirt. "May I help you?"

"My name is Chester Donovan. Jim Hale said y'all might be looking for bronc busters."

"Welcome to Laramie Cross Breed Ranch, Mr. Donovan. I'm Isa O'Toole, and we do need a handful of horses saddle broke."

"I've broken a few," responded Donovan.

"Well, come on in and have some coffee," I said with a motion for him to enter.

Donovan entered ahead of me. He paused, as he saw Morning Star pouring coffee into three cups set on the table. "Hale didn't mention that you had a squaw," he said upon taking a seat.

I'd learned long ago to hold my temper. "Mr. Donovan, meet my wife Awentia. Over there is our son,

Moses. Awentia is a Miniconjou Lakota, and I am half Penateka Comanche. Do you have a problem with that?"

Donovan smiled broadly. "No, sir. Hale did tell me. I guess I wanted to see whether you'd react like the man of faith he said you were. I hope y'all don't mind that I've killed a few warriors in battle."

"You a God-fearing man, Mr. Donovan?" I asked.

He nodded and took a sip of coffee. "Wow! Great coffee, ma'am."

"I've had to kill hostiles, and Awentia here has, too. It's a sad toll that evil exacts."

"That it be. Not sure there's really any winners," observed Donovan.

"We're raising Quarter Horses here bred with mustangs. We have some two-year-olds that need to be saddle broke. Have you saddle broken broncs?"

"Yes, sir. Did that a bit in Arkansas and Texas. Got the bruises and scars to prove it," he said with a chuckle.

"Do you reckon to stay with the 2nd Cavalry or leave?"

Donovan thought a moment. "Expect I'd like to see how this works out afore I decide."

I figured that was a solid answer. "Let's take you out and introduce you to some fine horseflesh."

He gave me a quizzical look.

"You can bring your coffee," I said with a smile. It was good coffee. With that, I stood and led him outside to the barn.

"We keep our mares in here as part of controlling the breeding process."

"You're ensuring consistency," said Donovan.

"Yes. Cowboys and ranchers buying our Quarter Horses will look for that."

"Size, gait, conformity, speed, and agility are bywords for us," I shared.

Donovan perched his coffee atop one of the stall stanchions and eased himself in beside a mare. He began examining her. "Right fine, Mr. O'Toole." He looked me in the eyes. "If I might say, you're right young for this business, yet you seem to know what you're doing. Do you know a fellow named Burt Wilkins?"

"Burt? Why, he's a friend of my pa and spent a couple of months up here helping me get started. You know him?"

"I worked with him a bit on the King Ranch," replied Donovan.

We walked out to the corral where a couple of two-year-olds were frolicking about. He eased himself inside the corral and began talking gently to the colts. In a matter of perhaps twenty minutes, the colts were nuzzling Donovan's hands and letting him stroke their necks and forelocks.

I must say that I was impressed. "We'd be pleased to hire you, Mr. Donovan. If borrowing you part-time from the 2nd Cavalry works out, we'll see about a greater commitment. We do have plans to have a second spread in Texas to raise cattle."

Donovan's eyes grew wide. "Y'all are ambitious," he exclaimed.

"You can park your equipment in yonder bunkhouse. We'll give you three squares when you're here. I daresay it'll be an improvement over cavalry grub. We're informal here, so feel free to call me Isa."

"Burt here," responded Donovan, and we shook hands.

I gave him a once-over. "You might consider wearing

something besides those military issue clothes. On the chance one of our horses tosses you...well, you know."

As we headed back to the house, Taabe appeared. Donovan did a double-take. "Hale mentioned the wolves, but I thought he was joking," he said, with jaw dropped in amazement.

"Taabe and his pack are added security," I explained.

"He's not going to attack me, is he?"

"Only if you came at me or my wife," I replied.

That seemed to satisfy Donovan, though he remained just a tad nervous.

"You'll get used to them," I assured him.

* * *

With our first actual hired hand, it felt as though we were truly a going enterprise. While we appreciated George's generosity in loaning Hap or Dred to us, the feeling of independence was welcome. We were pretty much self-sufficient. We'd soon be selling our Quarter Horses and hopefully turning a profit.

Now and then, Lieutenant Dickerson routed his patrols past our home. It was undoubtedly his way of showing his gratitude for having saved his life. Dickerson told us about the stubborn resistance of the Wallows Band of the Nez Percé under the great Chief Joseph. General Sherman had sent General Howard after the tribe. Some Nez Percé had escaped to Canada and joined with Sitting Bull's Lakota Sioux. A bit more than four hundred Nez Percé had already surrendered and been sent to Fort Leavenworth.

Word of Chief Joseph's surrender actually came from George Freeman. The mighty chief gave a surrender speech in which he was quoted as saying, "I will fight no more forever." It was a sad appendage to the plight of the Red man under the onslaught of American pioneers and accompanying military might.

Chapter 18

Horse Thieves?

It took all of about a month and a half for Donovan to saddle-break our colts. They were maturing into as fine a stock as any experienced cowboy could hope to have under his saddle. We now had seven branded and ready-to-ride Quarter Horses. There was no doubt in my mind that we were following God's plan for us. Given the current market for top-tier horseflesh, we anticipated selling them for better than three hundred dollars each.

We decided that the time had come to begin to make a profit from this horse breeding business. I had heard of horse trading going on far south of our Laramie Cross Breed Ranch down in Cheyenne. Apparently, ranchers driving cattle up the Western Trail had made the town a stopping off point on their way home. Flush with cash, they were seeking good horses. It was crucial that we meet this need before the onset of winter.

I was concerned for Morning Star's safety while we were gone, but she was confident that she could hold down the home front. I had to keep reminding myself that she was a battle-tested woman, a warrior wife.

Dickerson assured me that he'd increase patrols through the area and George would surely check now and then, but it still left me feeling uneasy. I wanted to rely on Taabe and his pack, but he was of his own mind as to whom his wolf instincts were attached.

"I be okay," she assured me. "Me strong woman."

I worried as to how strong she would perform against any serious attack. I had to take some small comfort in knowing that most Lakota and Cheyenne were now situated on reservations. The fight had been driven from their leaders.

The day of departure finally arrived. Hap, Donovan, and I cut out five of our Quarter Horses and prepared to lead them off to market. The horses wore halters and were strung on long tethers. They were saddle broken, but did have enough mustang in them that the tethers were a must. It was a four-day trek, but Morning Star had made sure that we were well-supplied. Most importantly, we were well-armed.

The country that lay ahead of us was not the roughest on the frontier, but it had its perils. Open grasslands were broken by hills and ravines. To our west, lay the Laramie Range. While its peaks were high, they were as nothing compared to what Morning Star and I had experienced on our journey to Yellowstone. There was no shortage of places for folks to lie in ambush.

To put it bluntly, we were a very attractive target. No self-respecting band of Indians could pass up our little herd. We tried our best to stay away from the tops of hills where we were easily silhouetted, instead riding just beneath the crests. Neither did we lead our horses through ravines, as we could be easily ambushed by warriors from above us. Ravines were especially indefensible positions regardless of cover.

We traveled through thinly populated country for the first two days. This was the most dangerous portion of our journey, and we wouldn't be disappointed. On the afternoon of the second day, my senses went on high alert.

I reined in at the sight of tracks made from unshod horses. I slid from my saddle and poked a finger in a horse dropping. It was warm. This signaled that the tracks were fresh. "Hap…Burt…look at these. Looks to be six hostiles. Given where we are, I'll bet they're most likely Arapaho."

We all drew our carbines as unobtrusively as possible. I now kept an eye out for places to defend against what was looking like an impending attack. It's an eerie, strange feeling to know that hostile eyes are watching and awaiting the optimal opportunity to lift your hair and take your horses.

"We need high ground," advised Donovan, drawing upon his military training.

My personal experience echoed that advice, though I recalled hearing that Custer had high ground at Little Bighorn. I spotted a thick stand of lodgepole pine ahead of us on a gently sloped hillside off to our right. We turned our route toward the trees gradually so as not to alert the hostiles regarding our intentions.

We no sooner arrived at the trees, when war whoops erupted from behind us.

"Hap, mind the horses!" I directed. It was all happening fast. By my count, there were seven of what appeared to be Arapaho. They were fully decked out in fighting gear. War paint served to give them spiritual strength and cause their enemies to be fearful. They were working up the courage to attack. Donovan and I both dismounted with our Spencer repeating carbines in hand. Hopefully, the savages wouldn't get close enough to bring my Colt revolver into the action. We both knew enough to wait until the enemy was within range.

Arrows and a smattering of ill-aimed gunshots came our way. Most of the gunfire fell short. The Arapaho were too excited by the prospect of prime horseflesh and their confidence in outnumbering us to be much concerned.

At about twenty-five yards with the hostiles bearing down upon us on lathered ponies laboring to gallop uphill, Donovan and I opened fire. Two Arapaho were shot from their ponies with our first salvo. The screaming of wounded horses and pained outcries of mortally wounded warriors filled the air. In but seconds, only two Arapaho remained unscathed. To our surprise, they bounded from their ponies and came at us, waving tomahawks. It was as though they were on a suicide mission. Just as the first savage came within ten feet of me and was about to throw his tomahawk, a shot from Hap dropped the warrior in his tracks. I spun with Colt in hand in time to stop the second attacker before he could reach Donovan. The hostiles had to have been insane. All lay about dead or dying. I thought back on stories my pa and ma had told me about tribal desperation and how powerful medicine men or shamans could convince warriors that they were immortal.

Donovan and I began reloading. It was second nature in Indian country and well that we did. A second wave of what I counted as eight Arapaho warriors appeared off to our right. They must have heard the melee and been lying in ambush up ahead. The same shaman must have cast a spell to convince them of their immortality, as they kicked their ponies to a gallop and came charging at us.

This was pure and certain insanity. The lifeless bodies of seven of their fellow warriors and at least three ponies laid around us. There was nothing immortal about them. I prayed silently that they would halt, give up their crazed intentions.

Donovan and I opened fire as soon as the savages were within range. Two were immediately unhorsed.

A fearsomely painted warrior with an elaborately decorated shield and feathered headdress, pulled up beyond the accurate range of our carbines. He shouted something that brought the remaining Arapaho to a halt. Had the horse thieves given up? More than half the band lay dead. The shaman's mystical assurances had not worked. The apparent leader waved his rifle at us in an apparent final act of defiance. Even from a distance, there was a sadness born of frustration and failure in the way he sat his pony. Perhaps Chief Joseph's final words of fighting no more would have been appropriate to him here. I turned to Donovan. "They're done for today, Chester." From what had happened, it was clear to me that the first attackers were to attack us on the trail and drive us into an ambush. When we headed for the trees, we disrupted their plan. The first attackers were committed nevertheless, and their blood rage drove them to attack. It was foolhardy and turned out terrible for them. Wives and children at home would now be fatherless.

Instinctively, I scanned around to be certain that there were no other hostiles. Who should I spy? Taabe. What went through my wolf companion's mind was beyond me. It was surely God's doing, as he and only two of his progenies had appeared in full view of the Arapaho and close enough for the savages to quickly recognize that we Whites were protected by strong medicine. Apparently, Taabe had left Mua and the rest of his pack behind at the ranch. I could only shake my head with wonder.

"How can you be sure?" Donovan asked.

"I'm half Comanche," I reminded him with an ironic smile. "They'll wait for us to leave, then gather their dead." I pointed to where Taabe stood. "And we had help."

Donovan nodded. "Your wolf friends are amazing." He turned to follow the retreating Arapaho. "Those Injuns were downright crazy. I fought Injuns before and never saw them so out of their minds," observed Donovan.

I simply nodded.

"Sad," added Donovan. "They are a beaten people."

With a deep sigh, I called to Hap. "We'd best be moving on. Hap, let's get out of here."

* * *

Cheyenne was booming. Sitting as it was on the route of the Union Pacific Railroad, its population had reached more than four thousand, and it had become a hub for both commercial and military operations.

We quickly learned that there were two primary horse-trading houses in Cheyenne. They were frequented regularly by ranch owners having recently sold off their herds following long drives up the Western Trail from Mexico and through Texas to as far north as Canada. There were also cowpokes with dollars left over from celebrating the end of those arduous trail drives and looking for a fine bronc. Both ranchers and drovers possessed what seemed like inbred appreciation for excellent horseflesh.

I wished Wilkins was with us, but Hap had pretty fair judgment, and Donovan was no slouch. My mountain cross brand stood out and earned questions from curious folks who'd yet to hear of the Laramie Cross Breed Ranch. The fact that both of my companions were a decade or more older, tended to make me appear younger than my seventeen years by contrast. In fact, I felt as though I was mostly being looked upon as the half-breed hired hand.

We selected a trading house and went to register my six Quarter Horses for sale.

The head livestock trader greeted us. He turned to Hap. "Welcome to the Cheyenne Livestock Auction House, home to the finest cattle and horses and best deals that can be had west of the Mississippi. I'm Sam Comstock." He stuck his paw out to Hap with a deferential look at me and a weak acknowledgment of Donovan.

Hap smiled. "Well, Mr. Comstock, Mr. O'Toole here has brought these fine cross-bred Quarter Horses here for sale to the right buyer. He be owner of the Laramie Cross Breed Ranch, where fine eastern thoroughbred Quarter Horses are bein' bred with hand-picked mustangs for strength, agility, an' speed."

Comstock turned to me with that all-too-common look I get when my long dark hair and high cheekbones brand me as half Indian. He did shake my hand. "Welcome, Mr. O'Toole," he said tentatively. "Mind if I have a look?" he asked as he walked over to my Quarter Horses. He took his time giving them a studied once-over.

I displayed the papers we had for each of our horses, and that touch of professionalism seemed to register appreciatively with him.

"How much you expecting from these fine Quarter Horses?" he asked forthrightly.

I tried to avoid a patronizing smile. What sort of fool did he think I was? I dared not ask. "These are exceptionally well-bred. They're all saddle broken. The question is, what do you reckon they'll fetch?"

My pa had counseled me to turn questions back on the questioner when negotiating. "I must admit that they are right fine, Mr. O'Toole." He rubbed his chin. "I can make you an offer here and now, or you can go to auction."

I knew that it was a time of year when most trail drives had been completed and money was to be had. "What sort of offer do you have in mind, Mr. Comstock?"

"Two hundred each," he said flatly.

I turned to Hap and Donovan. "Did you hear this man describe these Quarter Horses as fine?" I laid a puzzled expression on Comstock. "Surely you can do better. I'm sure you have personal knowledge of buyers that would be interested or are well aware that these horses will bring top dollar at auction...maybe as much as four hundred dollars. You surely can do better than three hundred each." I reckoned that if I could get three hundred, I'd avoid the trader percentage at auction. I wanted to be heading home from Cheyenne, and the sooner the better. It was too crowded for my tastes.

Comstock's eyes grew big, and there was a hint of anxiety-driven saliva in his mustache. He sure-as-shooting coveted my stock. "Two hundred seventy-five," he proposed. He obviously had trouble with three hundred dollars.

I glanced at Hap.

He gave a slight upward head nod.

"Two hundred eighty-five dollars each, and we have a deal, Mr. Comstock."

Comstock extended his hand. "I'll draw up the bills of sale."

I was soon the possessor of a bank draft for one thousand four hundred and twenty-five dollars. We promptly deposited it in the bank.

I felt a tad obliged to thank Hap and Donovan by way of celebrating before we headed home.

* * *

We headed north the next morning with Hap and Donovan hungover and desperately clinging to their saddles. We made several stops the first day while they tended to their personal needs. I thanked the Lord that we made for unappetizing targets for any wrongdoing.

As the sun reached its zenith on the third day of our ride home, with me scouting the trail about a hundred yards in front, I saw a sight that took my breath away. Little more than a hundred yards before me was the most incredibly beautiful bay-colored stallion with three mares, a foal, and a couple of colts. I slowly backed Paint and allowed Hap and Donovan to catch up to me. I put my finger to my lips to quiet them before they could say a word. "Look at that awesome stallion," I ventured.

Both men nodded silent affirmation.

"He be handsome," whispered Hap.

"You fixing to catch him, boss?" murmured Donovan.

I shook my head. "Not just yet. I expect he's not catchable. I think it will take gaining his trust," I observed. "It's going to take some time." I gazed at the big mustang as he ate while keeping a wary eye on us. "Y'all go wide around yonder trees, while I sit here a spell and get acquainted." I looked down at Taabe. "You go with them. I don't need this hoss worrying about protecting that foal."

Amazingly, Taabe gave me a measured look and followed Hap and Donovan.

* * *

I spent the next hour sitting atop Paint simply watching the stallion and his brood. I found myself totally taken with the horse. His dark color served to enhance the impact of the sunlight on his well-muscled frame. He was big and possessed great conformity.

Every now and then, he'd raise his head and take a long look at me. He was downwind, so was getting a pretty good whiff of my scent. He surely sensed that I wanted to meet him up close and personal, but he was a wary bit of horseflesh. He likely knew my intentions and was probably laughing at me inside.

So far as I could make out, he wore no brand. His natural wariness had apparently served him well as concerned anyone owning him. Surely, I wasn't the first human to covet him.

I eased Paint a couple of steps forward.

The big bay's head came up, ears went erect, nostrils flared, and his loud whinny sailed across the meadow that lay between us.

"I'll be back another day," I said to him and turned Paint to follow Hap and Donovan. I kept an eye on the bay stallion for as long as I could. It was reciprocated.

Just as I rode from his sight, I saw him nudge his brood away in the opposite direction from me. It was as if to say, *Lots of luck, cowboy.*

The image of that big bay stallion—my big bay stallion – hung with me for the remainder of the ride home.

Chapter 19

Kidnapped?

The landscape became ever more familiar as we journeyed nearer the Laramie Cross Breed Ranch. We'd managed a decidedly fruitful trip to Cheyenne and were returning with our scalps intact and pockets full of cash. I did pay Donovan and Hap for their help, though it was more of a bonus for Donovan, given that he was one of my hands.

It was around midday when I spotted my home off in the distance. I'd have pushed Paint to a gallop, but our horses were plumb tuckered. The ranch seemed strangely quiet as we approached. There was no movement of human or beast that I could make out. I stuck my heels into Paint's sides to hasten our arrival. He did his best to speed his tired legs into a canter. Hap's and Donovan's mounts did their level best to keep up.

Within fifty yards of the house, I could see that the front door was wide open. "Awentia!" I called out. "Awentia!" No response. Paint drew up as much from being tired as being repelled by a stench. As I leaped from my saddle, I saw two dead Arapaho savages. Their condition at first glance told me they'd likely been killed the previous day. I rushed inside the house, but there was no sign of Morning Star. I searched for an indication of a struggle. Nothing was out of place, except that Morning Star's Henry carbine was missing.

By this time, Hap and Donovan had pulled up along with Taabe.

My wolf friend was obviously distraught. He, too, sensed that something was dreadfully wrong.

Hap rode around to the back of the house and quickly returned. "There be two dead wolves back there an' a terribly mauled Arapaho," he announced.

Donovan's trooper experience kicked in, and he made his own investigation. He returned to tell us that the three Quarter Horse stallions were missing. "There's a mix of shod and unshod tracks heading southeast, Isa."

"How many?" I asked.

Donovan shrugged. He had fought many an Indian but never done any serious scouting or tracking.

I ran toward the barn with a well-lathered Paint following me. I scanned the area and saw the badly-mauled Arapaho. There looked to have been no more than five unshod ponies. Upon closely examining the hoofprints of the Quarter Horses, it appeared that one of them carried the extra weight of a rider. I reckoned that must be Morning Star. I also saw wolf tracks. Donovan had been correct as to the direction Morning Star had taken in her attempt to escape. The Arapaho were surely hot on her heels.

Taabe gave me a distressed look and let out a howl at finding the two dead members of his pack. Where were Mua and the rest? At his call, two wolves appeared, but not Mua. They nuzzled at each other, then took off on a run upon finding Mua's trail.

I called Hap and Donovan to join me. I had begun to put the pieces of the scene together in my mind.

"What do you think, boss?" asked Donovan.

"Looks as though Awentia defended herself and managed to escape. I'd guess that Mua and the wolves confused the Arapaho and gave her time to grab the stallions and escape. It looks as though she's riding one of the stallions and Mua is with her. I have a fair idea where she might be headed." I paused and took a long look at my two travel-weary companions. "Y'all don't have to go after her with me."

They both gave me *you shouldn't have to ask* looks.

"The Arapaho have a day's head start. Let's resupply quickly, get fresh mounts, and then head out." I paused. "Hap, how about you heading on to the Circled Cross and letting George know? If he and Dred want to join us, they can rendezvous at the rock cave about a day due south of the ranch." I was taking a truly wild guess as to where Morning Star was looking to hole up. I'd initially been surprised that she'd abandoned the house but figured she must have been intent on trying to save the stud horses. That she would try to save them while risking her own life bewildered me. Then again, she was a warrior.

Hap didn't hesitate. He nodded, saddled one of the mustangs in the corral, and was off to George's place.

Donovan and I resupplied with ammunition and food. I took Paint to the barn and made sure he was settled in, then we saddled fresh mounts and rode out. We had the good sense to bring two spare horses, as we figured to be riding hard.

By now, Taabe was well ahead of us. He hadn't lingered to mourn the loss of his pack.

I expected that Morning Star, riding the speedy and

durable Quarter Horses, was giving the Arapaho quite a chase. The Indian ponies were no match for her mounts, and she likely had the good sense to switch horses every few miles. She didn't weigh more than a hundred pounds, but changing horses gave the galloping cayuses a breather of sorts.

As the sun moved inexorably toward the horizon, Donovan and I found ourselves within sight of the place I rightly reckoned that Morning Star had chosen. It was a place we'd camped at, a rock outcropping that offered a wide field of view across a meadow that swept downward for a couple of hundred yards. There was plenty of space to hobble the horses and even a spring to provide water.

"Stay here, Chester. I'm going to do a little scouting. Cover my back." I dismounted to surveil the area surrounding Morning Star's makeshift fortress. I easily found the remuda of Arapaho war ponies but no immediate sign of the hostiles. I snuck a tad further toward where I figured them to be hiding. Then, one by one, I caught sight of an eagle feather here and another there, sticking above the sage bushes. They hid like cats with their bodies under cover but tails sticking out for anyone to see. Those feathers might as well have been cat tails. The hostiles respected Morning Star's Henry repeating rifle and were waiting her out. It was a siege, of course. Or was it a siege? Could they be awaiting reinforcements? I found my way back to Donovan.

"What's our plan?" asked Donovan. "I'd expect we could bring down a couple of the savages before they can react."

With no sign of George, Hap, and Dred, we were outnumbered. The hostiles were also spread out, which meant that a direct attack was very risky. "Too risky," I replied. "We'll wait for George." I prayed to my Lord that my Circled Cross friends would get here and soon. I worried that one of the savages might get brave and approach Morning Star from the rear of the outcropping and drop from above. The savage would have the advantage of surprise and challenge her to react in time. I tried to think of a way to let her know that we were here, but every option had considerable attendant risk.

"How are you with that pigsticker on your belt, Chester?"

"Whatcha thinking?" he asked.

"Comes darkness, maybe we can even the odds a bit and catch a couple of those warriors unawares." It was a dangerous tactic, but the Arapaho likely wouldn't realize their loss until daylight. With that thought, I heard a shot and then a scream from where I'd seen one of the hostiles. Morning Star was up to this fight. The odds might be improving.

I pointed out to Donovan the locations where I'd spotted the Arapaho attackers. I hoped and prayed they'd not moved. We waited patiently. Under a quarter moon, Donovan and I moved in on the hostiles.

We stalked stealthily with the painstakingly slow steps of a half-breed teen and a retired cavalry trooper turned ranch hand. I stepped straight ahead, while Donovan moved to my left. It took about an hour to close within about ten yards of my quarry. He was nicely silhouetted against the dim light of the starry sky. The hostile was facing away from me as he intently watched Morning Star's lair.

I heard what must have been Mua's howl from Morning Star's position. She had responded to something. It was followed by a snarl, and the Arapaho savage in front of me disappeared in a cloud of dust and fury. I heard the sickening sound of bones being crushed by the jaws of a hundred-seventy-pound wolf, coupled with the desperate scream of the victim. The noisy scuffle quite naturally alerted the other Arapaho warriors. I could only imagine the horror of hearing a brother warrior's dying screams in the dim blackness of the night. There was a rustling off to my right, and Taabe had quickly brought the jaws of death to a second savage.

I heard feet running for ponies.

"Chester?" I called out.

"I'm okay!" he responded. "One of them heathens ran right over me."

With the Arapaho on the run, I called out to Morning Star. "Awentia!" I hollered.

"Isa! Isa!" she hollered back.

I went running to the rock shelter and wrapped her in my arms.

"You found us!" she cried with relief. "I prayed you would remember this place."

I laughed. "I hoped this was where you would come. It was the only place I could think of that could be defended."

Donovan joined us. He was a bit dusty from having been knocked over, but otherwise was none the worse for wear.

Mua headed out to find Taabe. I could only imagine the grisly scene at which she'd find her mate and the rest of the pack. Taabe and the other two wolves had made short work of the two savages.

Once we'd had a chance to settle down, we had to decide what to do next. It wouldn't do to travel back to our house at night. We breathed easier, but were not yet out of danger. The embarrassed Arapaho might return with reinforcements.

"Let's wait until morning," I decided.

Donovan went out to fetch our horses. Even in the dim light, he looked decidedly pale upon his return.

"Something the matter, Chester?" Morning Star queried sympathetically.

"I passed what was left of one of the Arapaho," he said with a gag.

I reckoned that I'd better change the subject. "Maybe George will arrive. He knows this place." I did want to head back to our house as quickly as possible.

We settled in for a long, chilly night. Chilly because we decided it was best to not build a fire that would tell the world where we were.

* * *

Just as the golden glow of the sunrise painted the eastern horizon, George and Hap arrived. Our shelter instantly became overcrowded. We gratefully made space.

"Thanks for coming, George," I said while enduring one of his bearish hugs.

"I brought some grub that Running Waters wouldn't let us leave without," he said.

We were all hungry, so we didn't hesitate to dig in.

"Where's Dred?" I asked.

"Sent him on to Fort Laramie. I thought we might need some cavalry." George's words were spouted with the confidence of a man who knew his way in the frontier west. The blue coats would be welcome if the Arapaho did indeed return.

As the sun rose higher, we prepared to head home. About the time I threw my saddle on the mustang I'd ridden from the ranch, I glanced over my cayuse's back. My eyes popped wide, and I swallowed hard. There must have been at least two dozen mounted Arapaho warriors preparing to attack us. They were painted up fiercely and wore full battle regalia. "Look!" I hollered, pointing to the force arrayed before us.

We faced a serious problem. Morning Star ran to my side. "What we do?"

"We pray that Dred is leading the cavalry our way." I hugged her and turned to George, Hap, and Donovan. "Looks like we'd best dig in," I observed. There didn't seem to be much else we could do. Perhaps, the good news was that the Arapaho wanted those prized Quarter Horse stallions, so they wouldn't risk firing salvos of arrows and bullets at us. To win, they would have to overrun us. Unfortunately for us, they had the numbers to do it. We had a weapons advantage with our repeating rifles, but those odds could be evened all too quickly.

I watched them remove the gruesome remains of their dead Arapaho brothers. They were taking their sweet time, but would soon muster the courage to attack.

"They'll attack directly from the front," I temporized. "That will be a diversion."

I received curious looks.

"Diversion?" asked Hap.

"They're going to drop into our laps from above," I said with full confidence.

"You're likely right," agreed Donovan.

"While we're trying to pick off moving targets before us, a bunch will come at us from above." I then repeated the tactic for their benefit, but it was as if to convince myself that it made sense. "I expect we ought to pray," I urged.

Hap kept watch while the rest of us prayed that we'd survive the inevitable attack.

I'd overheard folks back in Texas tell my pa that they always saved a bullet for themselves rather than face the tortures Indians inflicted upon their captives. Suicide, no matter the reason, seemed wrong to me. It was a sin and a cowardly escape. So far as I was concerned, I'd go down fighting to my last breath. Yes, Indian tortures were horrible, and Pa had warned me of some of the excruciatingly painful evils the savages were capable of inflicting on a human body. He said it was wrong, but he taught me that evil folks around the world had stooped to such moral lows against their enemies for centuries. This day, here in Wyoming, the savages would not have the opportunity to exact such perversity.

The sun reached its midday position high above. The Arapaho hostiles chanted as they strove to muster the courage to launch an assault upon us. They'd already lost five warriors to Morning Star and to Taabe's pack, so they undoubtedly realized that they faced strong *sunipu*. The wolf was of special concern, as it represented great spiritual strength.

The tension was finally broken by a great chorus of whoops and shouts. From below, at least fifteen hostiles came charging up toward us, waving warclubs, tomahawks, and spears. They were making enough noise to awaken the dead. We fired as fast as we could. There was no shortage of targets. Wounded and dying warriors and horses screamed, wailed, and bawled, but survivors still came on. The frontal attack meant that the remaining savages must have circled around behind and above us. By the time the frontal assault was no more than fifty feet from us and the Arapaho were eating plenty of lead from our carbines, eight fearsomely painted hostiles dropped on top of us. Their blood-curdling yelling announced their arrival.

Having figured out what the hostiles were up to, I was mostly ready. I swung out with my knife at an Arapaho warrior that had landed directly in front of me, slicing a deep gash across his chest before he could gain his balance and have a chance to swing his warclub. The pain inflicted by my Bowie knife caused him to drop his weapon.

I saw Morning Star fell one savage with a hip shot from her carbine. She immediately levered another round and turned on another Arapaho warrior.

By this time, the remaining warriors from the frontal assault were nearly upon us. I saw Hap fall from a warclub to his head. George was bleeding from an arm wound but holding his own, wrestling with a hostile nearly as big as him.

The Arapaho losses were heavy, but they were intent on delivering their insane savagery and getting those prized Quarter Horses.

Taabe and his pack went to work on the warriors attacking our frontal defenses. They were learning that their fears of the mighty wolf were justified. The very sound of the snarling wolves and snapping bones ought to have weakened any sane human's resolve, but the Arapaho were committed to this battle. The frontal assault pressed on, and our makeshift fortress became a place of sweaty, bloody, writhing bodies in a clash to the death.

The mortally wounded Arapaho still stood in my face. His heaving chest pressed close to mine, as I worked my blade up between us and plunged my knife up to its hilt under his chin. Quickly bathed in the savage's blood, I let him slip from my grasp. I felt the hot breath of another Arapaho behind me. I turned. All went black.

Epilogue

The American western frontier was mostly unforgiving, a meeting of savagery and civilization. More and more towns were springing up, and they served as bellwethers to the civilizing of the frontier. *The Frontier Calls: Two Spirits, One Adventure* offers a peek into the courage, faith, endurance, and pure grit entailed in the conquest of the west. I decided at age fifteen that it was time to venture out on my own. Little did I know that the Great Plains Indian Wars loomed ahead. I'm seventeen now with a warrior woman wife, a child, and raising Quarter Horses in Wyoming. The world around me was a mix of the natural beauty of a rugged landscape and lurking dangers. This environment seemed to attract the best and worst of humans.

Life expectancy on the frontier was nothing like today. A male Indian did well to live beyond age thirty, and women could expect to live a tad less. Little wonder that older tribesmen were highly respected. Life expectancy for Whites wasn't much better. A White man on the frontier tended not to live beyond his late thirties.

Notably, the brevity of life generally meant that folks had to mature sooner. By the time a man or woman reached age fifteen or sixteen, he or she was pretty much an adult in terms of others expecting him or her to carry an adult set of responsibilities.

Indians? I am half Comanche. While I've dealt with Kiowa, Arapaho, Crow, Cheyenne, Shoshone, and Ute, most of my experience has been with the Comanche and Lakota peoples. Dangers? Anthropology-minded folks claim there were as many as thirteen distinct tribes of Comanche from the Quahadi or "antelope eaters" in the north to the Penateka or "honey eaters" in the south. Mix in Kiowa, Apache, and Tonkawa, and settlers had their hands full. The very name Comanche loosely translates in the Ute tribal language as *kumantsi* or "enemy." Capture by the Comanche invariably led to terrible outcomes. A fearsome lot these tribes were. The horse, coupled with a long history of trade for the latest weapons and farm-grown foods in and around the Comancheria, produced a highly aggressive nomadic culture heavily dependent on the buffalo. For example, Penateka Comanche Chief Buffalo Hump led more than 600 warriors on a raid through the heart of Texas in August 1840, murdering Texans, looting the city of Victoria, and looting and burning Linnville on their march to the Gulf of Mexico. It was not until 1858 that Texas Ranger John Salmon "Rip" Ford led the force of 102 heavily armed Texas Rangers and 100 Indian allies that brought the Comanche to their knees at the Battle of Little Robe Creek on the Canadian River in Oklahoma as described in my pa's Frontier Chronicle *Warpath: Jack's Faith is Tested.*

The northwestern plains were peopled by many tribes but especially the Sioux, comprised of three groups: Dakota, Nakota, and Lakota. The Lakota were made up of seven subgroups: Oglalas (famed for Red Cloud and Crazy Horse), Hunkpapas (famed for Sitting Bull), Miniconjous (People Who Live Near Water), Oohenunpas (Two Kettles), Itazipacolas (No Bows), Brulés (Burnt Thighs), and Sihásapas (Blackfeet). The Lakota history was no less combative than Comanche or Cheyenne. Despite the violence of the frontier, it's notable that the Lakota held to a worthy set of virtues, especially generosity, courage, fortitude, and wisdom. The North Platte country referred to in *The Frontier Calls: Two Spirits, One Adventure* was part of the Wyoming Territory established in 1868.

There were plenty of wild animals on the frontier. I do refer to bison as buffalo. Just for the record, bison and buffalo are quite different. Visualize the water buffalo and then the shaggy, awkward bulk of the American bison. Seems that "buffalo" came into common usage in America to refer to the bison, so I've chosen to use buffalo in my writings. Notable, too, is that the evasive four-legged critter many unwary folks refer to as an antelope is properly called a pronghorn. Catch one if you can. There is also a big predatory cat that most folks in North America call a mountain lion, but also answers to puma, cougar, or panther.

Historically notable in the Wolf's Tales is that the longest and most used cattle trail was the Great Western Trail from 1874 to 1893. It ran from Matamoros, Mexico, to Val Marie, Canada. As many as three hundred thousand cattle each year would eventually be driven up that Great Western Trail, especially by the likes of famed rancher Charles Goodnight.

I enjoyed no modern creature comforts. The invention of telephones was decades into the future. Transportation? Horses, mules, and oxen—ridden or pulling wagons—were the vehicles of choice. I enjoyed no refrigerator to preserve sweet treats. There were no flush toilets or showers. Folks mostly ate what grazed upon or grew from the land. Learning was squeezed from the few books that might be found, especially the Holy Bible. Can't say as the living of the era was luxurious unless you counted the sheer grandeur of majestic landscapes and of nights so quiet you could hear the stars twinkling. To fully appreciate the place, you simply had to love the incredible beauty of the outdoors. Fishing the meandering Guadalupe River in Texas or the chill waters of Wyoming's North Platte River, taking in the grandeur of Yellowstone National Park, hunting deer and pronghorn, raising cattle and horses, and reaping the bounteous yield of the rich soil was sheer joy for a courageous visionary few. For a teen on the frontier, life could be pretty good…mostly. Otherwise, it was downright dangerous.

Thus far, I was quickly growing to manhood. My vision quest had led me on a path known only to God. I was striving to conquer personal fears and prejudices, fight Indians and bandits, defend against wild beasts, travel the wild country, and drive cattle and horses. With it, I found the love of my life and a life purpose. As you have seen, I especially draw upon my faith and what I was taught by my parents. And yet, all of this is constantly tested. I had to learn to trust in instincts forged from my biblical and life lessons. Yes, I'm on a frontier adventure and more. And you, dear reader, will now be able to follow me, Isa O'Toole, as I seek my own way in life and share my adventures. May God ever bless me and Morning Star.

Glossary

Definitions

Bear sign—Cowboy slang for donuts.

Big Father or Great Father—All-powerful Indian deity.

Bota bag—A canteen fashioned from leather and popular among Indians, mountain men, and many travelers of the western frontier.

Cold Camp—Camp without a campfire, generally done to avoid the smoke that might alert threats.

Dog run—The sheltered space or breezeway between two sections of some southern ranch houses. Living quarters were usually on one side and sleeping quarters on the other.

Fletch—The fin-shaped bird feathers on an arrow that help stabilize its flight.

Gallery—A synonym for porch. Folks in the West often called the structures across the front of their homes galleries.

Life debt—A cultural phenomenon in which

someone whose life is saved or spared by another becomes indebted or in some way connected to their savior.

Pemmican—Lean dried strips of meat pounded into a paste, mixed with fat and berries, and then pressed into small cakes.

Possibles bag (aka parfleche)—A leather or canvas sack carried by cowboys and containing essentials like soap, matches, bandages, extra spurs, smoke makings, and playing cards

Remuda—A herd of horses frequently deployed on trail drives and by Plains Indians.

Rendezvous—Annual celebratory gathering of mountain men.

Sand—Courage.

Shaman—Medicine man.

Teepee—An enclosed conical transportable shelter constructed of long poles and buffalo hides with a vent at the top to permit smoke to escape.

Travois—A wedge-shaped structure constructed of two poles and a cross-beam lashed together and dragged behind horses, mules, or dogs by Plains Indians.

Wahg!—Mountain man version of hail the camp or hello.

COMANCHE TRANSLATIONS

Aitu—Not good

Ana o'a hi'it—Phrase for "desire to eat"

Ap—Father

Aruka—Deer

Eetu—Bow

Ekakwitsubaitu—Lightning

Ekapitu—Red

Eekasahpana paraiboo—Army officer (soldier chief)

Haa—Yes

Hawokatu—Hollow, loose

Hoikwa—Hunt, look for prey

Isa—Wolf

Isa wasu—Poison

Kaahaniitu—deceive, cheat

Kahni—Life

Kamakuna—Loved one

Kee—No

Kobe—Wild horse

Kohto—Build a fire

Kooitu—Die

Kuhmabai—Married

Kuisa—Coyote

Kuuna—Fire

Kuya akatu—Afraid of

Kwakuru—Defeat someone

Kwihnai—Eagle

Mua—Moon

Mukue—Spirit

Nahuu—Knife

Natsuitu—Strong

NiyáŋkA—We eat

Numu—Cow, Cattle

Numunahkahnis—Family

Numunuu—Referring to the members of the Comanche tribes. Literally: people.

Ohapitu—Yellow

Onaa—Son or daughter

Paa—Water

Pabi—Friend

Paaka—Arrow

Peeka—Kill

Pia—Mother

Pia huutsuu—Bald eagle

Pia wa'óo—Comanche words for mountain lion, puma, or cougar.

Pihi—Heart

Pohya (or poya)—Walk

Puuka—Horse

Sunipu—Medicine (as in strong medicine)

Suumaru—Ten

Taa Narumi—Master; God

Taabe—Sun

Tabu—Coward

Tamu—Rabbit

Tasiwoo—Buffalo

Tenahpu—Man

Tomoobi—Sky

Tosa—White man or woman

Tosaabitu—White

Tumah tuyai—After life

Tuhibitu—Black

Tumhyokenu—Believe, trust

Tu Taiboo—Black man

Umaru—Rain

Unha haksi nahniaka—Phrase for *what's your name?*

Wa'ipu—Woman

Wasápe—Bear

Wutsutsuki—Rattlesnake

LAKOTA TRANSLATIONS

Ate—Father

Ayústan—Abandon, retreat, leave

Enákiya—Stop

Hau, mitákuye oyás'e—Welcome

Igmuwatogla—Mountain lion

Ínyan—Fire

Isan—Knife

Iya Tate—Wind

Iyaya—Go, leave

Jiji—Light hair

Katá—Kill

Kola—Friend (male)

Kize—Fight

Maka—The earth and grandmother of all things

Mas'óphiye—Trade or barter

Mato—Bear, also eat

Mini—Water

Nagi—The spirit that has never been a man

Nanji—Jealous

Niya—Ghost

Okin—Pretty

Oyate—The people or nation

Sapa—Black

Ska—White

Scan—Sky

Sunkawaka—Horse

Sunkmanitu tanka—Wolf

Takuwe—Why

Tanka—Wolf

Tatanka—The great beast (patron of health, ceremonies, provision)

Unk—Created by Maka; embodies all evil beings

Unktehi—One who kills

Wakan Tanka—God (monotheistic)

Wamaka nagi—Animal spirit

Wanbli—Eagle

Wani—Four winds (weather)

Wasake—Strong

Wash tay—Good
Wasichus—White man
Wasna—Pemmican
Wi—The sun (chief of all gods)
Wica—Complete man
Wicasa—Man (gender)
Wicasa wakan—Shaman
Wiiya—Danger
WiiyakA—Marry
Wiiyuka—Coward
Wiiyukta—Love
Winyan—Woman
Wowahwa—Peace
Zuzeca—Snake

Thank You

Thank you for taking the time to read *The Frontier Calls: Two Souls, One Adventure.* If you enjoyed it, please consider telling your friends or posting a short review. Word of mouth is an author's best friend and much appreciated.

Thank you.
Mark Greathouse

Watch For: Wild Horses on the Laramie: A Life of No Boundaries

(The Wolf's Tales 3)

AVAILABLE MARCH 2026

Want to make sure you don't miss the release? Sign up for our newsletter at **wisewolfbooks.com/newsletter**

Acknowledgments

Authoring books doesn't simply happen in a vacuum. The author provides the creative talent and crafts the stories, but there's so much more that demands acknowledgment. There are lots of folks and places that contribute to my authoring endeavors. So it is with *The Frontier Calls: Two Spirits, One Adventure.* The tale is set in 1876 and transitions to 1878, sharing the trials and tribulations of a young man forced to meet the challenges inherent in the dangerous vastness of the western frontier. But this novel stands apart. At its core, it is also about the taming of that frontier. The protagonist epitomizes the freedom of America's western frontier and represents a final bastion of honor in America. This tale follows Jack O'Toole's earlier Frontier Chronicles series beginning with his adventures in *Perilous Trails: Jack's Adventure Begins.* Hopefully, readers will find this second book in the Wolf's Tales series worthy of their time and emotional involvement. Saddle up and ride into the future with Isa O'Toole.

I've been blessed with many friends and family who have supported my writings. My wife Carolyn's reviews and encouragement were a huge help along with very important tech support from our sons Mike and Matt. Thanks to my pastor, Randy, for his faith insights. Many more friends and family have contributed support at some level to the creation and publication of my Wolf's Tales, be it encouragement or advice.

Naturally, I am major grateful to the great folks at the Wise Wolf Books imprint of Wolfpack Publishing. The team they bring to publishing is first-rate in editing, cover design, and the myriad tasks that lead to successful book sales.

It's only right to acknowledge my ancestors. They were actual settlers of the South Texas frontier. In addition to inspiring me, they provided a quite helpful true-to-life framework as to the life and times on the Texas Nueces Strip. I've also personally walked the very landscapes traversed by my fictional and historical characters.

Most of my authoring has occurred in my office as decorated to channel my inner Texan, but my creative juices have often been inspired and imagination stoked in cafés and coffee houses across America. My favorites were Hester's Café & Coffee Bar in Corpus Christi, TX; Nueces Café in Robstown, TX; Java Ranch Espresso Bar & Café in Fredericksburg, TX; PAX Coffee & Goods in Kerrville, TX; Ragged Edge Coffee House and Bantam Coffee Roasters in Gettysburg, PA; 1889 Coffee House in Helena, MT; Wild Joe's Coffee Shop, Bozeman, MT; Tumbleweed Café, Gardiner, MT; Dunn Brothers Coffee in Rapid City, SD; Postmasters Coffee & Bakery and Brio Coffeehouse in Waynesboro, PA; Birdie's Café and American Ice Co Café in Westminster, MD; Deja Brew Coffee House, New Oxford and Deja Brew at Miney Branch, Carroll Valley, PA; Baltimore Coffee & Tea Co., Frederick Coffee Company & Café, and Dublin Roasters in Frederick, MD; Qualle Café and Grounded Coffee & Bakery, Cherokee, NC; Palace Café, Amarillo, TX; and Unto Others Café, Lamar, CO. I must admit to also frequenting a few Dunkin Donuts and Starbucks around our fine nation. The décors and easy listening music in these fine establishments, combined with savory cups of coffee, tended to set me in the right creative frame of mind. They also afforded engagement with many fine citizens of our nation.

Last but not least, I'm especially thankful for the many folks who have read and enjoyed my books.

I do believe it's important to acknowledge how the old west represents the brave pioneering spirit of settlers who met the challenges and transcended mere survival to enable America to achieve exceptional growth. The settling of the American frontier west is replete with tales of leveraging freedom for individual achievement. I hope you'll agree that reliving our past—even through history-based fiction—often has the effect of pointing the way to an ever-brighter future. Might we be up to it? I hope that the inspiration I've drawn from my having walked the very earth my characters have trodden, coupled with my extensive historical research, will enable readers to fully experience the grit, adventure, and passion of my characters while sensing aromas of gunsmoke, trail dust, leather, and bluebonnets.

Thanks kindly to all of you, and please do enjoy *The Frontier Calls: Two Spirits, One Adventure.*

About the Author

Award-winning author Mark Greathouse's love for the western genre draws upon his deep family roots and love of the outdoors honed from teen years hiking the Appalachian Trail and family travels across America's frontier. Greathouse began writing full time after a successful career as a business executive and later as an entrepreneurial investor and advisor. His service as president of several business and community nonprofits led to their extraordinary growth. He holds a BA in English and MBA in marketing. Greathouse donates time and books annually to support wounded military warriors.

A member of Western Writers of America and the Wild West History Association, he also contributes articles on the history of America's west to western-themed magazines. Greathouse was recognized as a 2024 Finalist in western genre by the American Literary Book Awards for his sixth Tumbleweed Saga, *Nueces Truth: Texans Face War's Realities.*

His *Frontier Chronicles,* a series of western novels aimed at adventure-minded teens and young adults while weaving a Christian message within their fabric, are aimed at lighting fires of truth, faith, hope, and life purpose in the bellies of today's teen boys and girls. Just as seeds must be sown to reap the harvest, so the seeds of faith must be planted to raise tomorrow's men and women.

www.ingramcontent.com/pod-product-compliance
Lightning Source LLC
LaVergne TN
LVHW091126080826
845145LV00008B/2065

* 9 7 8 1 9 6 8 7 3 3 3 3 9 *